TRAP'N 4 CASH

TIGGA

Trap'n 4 Cash Copyright 2021 by TIGGA
ISBN: 978-0-9990847-5-5
Book Cover design and formatting by
www.ebooklaunch.com

Contact Information:
Lost and Found Publishing
PO Box 1032
Macon, GA 31201

www.Lostandfoundpub.com

Email: varjr@lostandfoundpub.com

Follow us on social media:
Lost_andfoundpub@instagram.com
Lostandfoundpublishing@facebook.com

Lost & Found Publishing

CHAPTER 1

RELOCATE

"What do you mean he's dead?" cried Michelle, trying to wrap her mind around the idea that her friend was gone. She couldn't understand how this stranger could just pop up on her doorstep with such terrible news.

Trap could tell by the look on her face that she was not taking Cash's death good, but it was necessary. He had instructions to follow, and as God as his witness, he planned on following them.

"Baby girl, I'm sorry you had to find out like this, but I was able to speak to him for a minute before he passed. That's why I am here."

"Wha- wha- what do you mean?" she asked, clearly confused about where this conversation was going.

"Look ma," he said making sure he had her attention, "cuzz told me to come by here and give you this." He pulled the Tom Ford book bag from his shoulder and passed it to her.

For a minute, she stood there in her doorway bewildered about what was going on. What was in the bag? And why was it so important for Cash to make sure she got it? Those were the questions that ran through her mind.

Noticing the lost expression on her face, Trap said "Open!"

When she looked inside, all she could see was a lot of Benjamin Franklin's staring back at her. It made her heart skip a beat, because it was the most money she'd ever had in her possession. Looking up from the money, she noticed Trap's awakening smile.

"That's for you ma, compliments from my man Cash," he cheerfully informed her.

"Oh my God!" she exclaimed, shocked. "How much is this?"

"A hunnid bands," he stated proudly, knowing that Cash was blessing her with a stack for every brick she unknowingly held for them. "Listen to me though," he continued, "he also told me to come pick up his Charger and let you know the money is for you to get another car."

She had completely forgotten about her vehicle after hearing the tragic news about her friend. It moved her, though, to know that he was thinking about her during his last few moments alive.

"Well, thank you for carrying out his wishes Mr..." she said, trying to remember his name.

"Trap," he said, finishing her statement.

"I'm sorry," she blushed from the embarrassment of forgetting his name.

"It's okay ma, I completely understand," he said, realizing how cute she was when she smiled. She was a real cute girl with a nice shape, so it wasn't hard for him to see how she caught his homie's attention.

"So, where is my car?" she asked out of curiosity.

"Let me just put it like this ma, they're both in a better place now, so when the insurance company calls, you tell them that a friend of yours borrowed the car and that's all you know, okay?"

She nodded her head as if she understood him completely.

Before she began asking any more questions, he spoke up, "I'm sorry to be in such a rush ma, but I'm gonna need those car keys from you now."

She apologized again before taking off to retrieve the keys from her bedroom. When she returned, Trap was standing in her front yard directing a flatbed truck into her driveway.

"Trap!" she shouted, trying to get his attention. He turned around and walked back over to where she was standing on her front porch.

"You know there's nothing wrong with it, right?" she asked, assuming he didn't know it was drivable.

"Yeah, I know," he said, answering her question, "but who's gonna drive my car?" He pointed across the street to where his Royal Blue Lamborghini was parked.

She couldn't believe her eyes. Everything she'd seen in the past 30 minutes told her that Cash was somebody she wished she'd gotten to know better.

"I appreciate your time Michelle and try not to spend all that money in one place, alright!"

Once the Charger was loaded onto the truck, Trap hopped into his Lambo and followed it. He was going to make sure that it made it to where it needed to go in order for him to strip it down and remove the 100 keys of coke they had stashed inside of it.

***

"What's wrong baby?" she barely whispered to Cash as she leaned over him and noticed the uncomfortable look on his face. He looked into her eyes and thanked God for blessing him with such a wonderful woman. Through all the mayhem that had occurred lately, he was shocked to see that she was still there by his bedside. Jasmin had proven to be the epitome of a ride or die chick, and he loved her from the bottom of his heart.

Here he was, laying in a bed with tubes connected to his body to ensure that he made a full recovery. It had only been a week since the green light to take him and his family out had been issued by the cartel. He had been fortunate enough to pull through, but only after being pronounced deceased by the doctor who operated on him for his gunshot wound to the chest and his traumatic head injury. However, although he survived, his little brother would not be so lucky.

Armani, aka Money, was pronounced DOA when the paramedics first arrived on the scene following the fatal assault that took place on him and Cash. He was now considered a memorable legend to the streets he once ran and grew up in, never to be forgotten by those who loved him and his brother the most. On street corners across Macon, and many other parts of Georgia, you would see t-shirts with the two brothers on it who started one of the most recognized organizations in the Peach State's history. Cash and Money were truly loved, respected, and honored for their loyalty to the streets.

"Man, those were my niggas dawg!"
"Yeah, we lost some real soldiers this time fam!"
"They don't make 'em like that anymore."

Those were just some of the cry's members of their crew and people who knew of them pled after hearing they were dead. However, contrary to what everyone heard on the streets, Cash was not dead. He was not the lost soul that they feared to be one of the victims to a game that played by no rules. No, not him. He was very much alive and very much ready to get back in the game that had turned its back on him.

Turns out, once Cash's loved ones were informed that he had in fact pulled through, Trap began strategizing on what moves to make for him and his crew. He knew that whoever wanted Cash and Money dead would not like the fact that one of them had actually survived the assassination attempt. He knew once the streets got a whiff of his survival, the madness would proceed to continue.

He had gotten word from one of his Lieutenants that the hit had come from Texas, but before he could react and seek revenge, he needed to hear from his best friend and co-partner, who was really responsible for bringing the drama to their doorstep, and why?

In the meantime, once the doctor stabilized Cash's condition, Trap ordered for all of his most loyal men to come upstairs for a private meeting. He told them to spread the word around town that Cash and Money had both been killed, and that there would be no revenge sought because the heads of their organization were now gone. So, as instructed by their boss, they hit the block and delivered the devastating news as if it was the gospel, and boy did the streets scream bloody Jesus.

Radio Stations, Club DJs, and local store owners all expressed their love for the two fallen soldiers who had contributed so much to their community. Mr. Mac, Cash's old boss, even threw a going away party for the two at his detail shop in remembrance of the two young men he considered his own sons.

Trap went as far as to having a funeral for the two brothers who were supposed to be eternally resting in their closed casket, along with their homie Scrappy and his grandmother whose bodies were too badly burnt to be exposed to the public. It was definitely not good news for the streets of Macon, but it was what it needed to stop the bloodshed.

Now, only a day after the funeral of his childhood friend and his grandmother, Cash was preparing to have a real funeral for his little brother Money.

Trap paid all the staff on Cash's hospital floor five thousand a piece to keep their mouths shut about his survival so he could keep him safe. Then, he had every piece of medical equipment moved down to the safe house in Richmond Hill, Georgia, so that Cash could make a full recovery, quietly. For most of the week, Jasmin stayed by his side to comfort and aid him.

She wanted to take care of him. She was his guardian angel and the love of his life, and every time he opened his eyes from resting and see her beautiful angelic face, his heart did backflips.

She was currently trying to get him ready for his brother's funeral, which was to be held on a lot in the back of their safe house. Money would be the first in their family to be laid to rest there, creating their own graveyard for their immediate family.

"Baby tell me what's wrong?" Jasmin begged, trying to figure out why he was rubbing around the bullet wound in his chest.

"It itches," he strained to whisper.

"Okay then boo, just hold on," she said, reaching over to the table next to his bed to grab his medication.

Trap hired a private medical staff to tend to Cash's wounds, but Jasmin constantly cussed them out for getting in her way. She felt like she was the only one that should be nursing him back to health. She would instruct staff members to tell her how to replace and change his bandages so that she could make sure he was being properly taken care of. She bathed him when he needed to be cleaned, changed his bed pan when he had to relieve himself, and fed him when he was hungry. Even Mercedees and Ms. Tina were having a hard time getting a chance to spend time with their beloved family member. Between Jasmin's attitude and the snub nosed .38 revolver she kept tucked away in her purse, they were not trying to get in-between the love she had for her man.

"Is that better baby?" she asked, rubbing the cream the doctor gave her around his chest wound to keep it from itching. "Yeah, that's perfect babe," he replied, smiling in response to her pampering.

He was still weak and could barely move, but with her around, there wasn't too much he couldn't do.

After dressing and grooming him, she laid him back down on his medical bed and called for the nurse who was on call to come help her push him towards the back of the house. It had been set up for them to have a private funeral session for Money, and Cash was intending on being there to see his brother off. As Jasmin and the nurse maneuvered his bed throughout the mini-mansion, armed bodyguards helped escort them towards the back, onto a screened—in porch. The guards lifted Cash's bed up and placed it on the walkway leading all the way to the back where the funeral was to be held.

As Jasmin continued pushing him, she took in all the nice smiles that greeted her along the way. Every single one of the 25 guests, including Ms. Tina, Mercedes, and a few other selected members of their crew could see the tiredness in her eyes. She had been there almost 24 hours a day, by his side to make sure that he pulled through. She was his strength, his motivation, and his backbone, and everyone knew it.

Cash was taking in the whole scene. As he looked upon some of the faces of his men, he felt proud. They were there to protect him with their own life, and he greatly appreciated their loyalty. As Jasmin pushed his bed towards the front, he smiled at how his mother and sister decorated the backyard. On both sides of the blue carpet were three rows of fold out chairs with his brother's picture on the back of them. There were white roses hanging on stands all over the place, which gave the backyard a peaceful serene setting. In the front was his brother's casket, which was next to a podium with a big picture of him and his son, after he was born.

When Jasmin guided him to the front and stopped, he looked over and saw Shay sitting there with his nephew AJ, Armani Junior, sitting next to her. She was too busy staring at the casket to realize he was looking at her. She was dressed in an all black Versace dress with her hair tied to the back in a bun. Her mascara was black and was slowly beginning to run down her tear-streaked face.

Cash felt sorry for her. He knew she loved his brother and to be without him made her days seem long and her nights seem even longer. If only she knew why they were even in this predicament in the first place, she probably wouldn't even be so messed up right now. However, Cash made it his business to make sure Trap cleaned up all the bad bloodwork that could have been exposed about Money in his autopsy.

"Hello everyone, let me start off by saying that we are all here to say our goodbyes to our beloved Armani and wish him well on his trip to the afterlife."

The preacher at the podium was beginning to give the eulogy and everyone took their seats. Cash did his best to sit up and pay attention, but the only thing that kept running through his mind while the preacher spoke, was the last few moments him and his brother shared hugging each other before the car they were in got riddled with bullets.

As he glanced over at AJ and saw how much he was beginning to resemble his father, Cash vowed to himself never to forget them last few moments he shared with Money.

***

"Did y'all find it or what?" Trap asked his two little partners, Damage and Tru. "Yeah," answered Tru, "but what do you want us to do with it?"

Trap had been sitting in his car waiting on them in McDonald's parking lot. He had instructed the both of them to go to Scrappy's grandma house, or what was left of it, and grab the safe from the basement. He wasn't so sure if it was still going to be there or not, but after speaking with Cash about it, he decided to put his two little soldiers on the job.

Now, after hearing the news that put the ball back in their court, he had to make a really big decision. From what Cash told him, they had approximately 2.5 million still left in the safe and if they were to be able to retrieve, it would be a big help. They both knew they had to relocate and start over, because if Manny got word that Cash was still alive, all hell would break loose.

Once Cash was able to speak again, filling Trap in on what had transpired causing the war, they would be able to address the matter. But until then, Trap wanted to seek revenge on Manny, Negro, and Migo himself. They still had a large amount of money to pull it off, but Cash knew that it wouldn't be wise to assassinate key members of a cartel. That would be the equivalent of the Japanese bombing Pearl Harbor all over again. He knew their resources only stretched so far, so he wasn't about to send his troops on a kamikaze mission.

"Look," he said, grabbing their attention, knowing exactly what to do next, "y'all take it out there to East Dublin and drop it off with Tameka, and then y'all come back to the Mac, alright."

"So, you don't want us to open it?" Damage asked him, curiously wanting to know what was inside, or rather, how much.

Trap looked at the both of them and gave it a second thought.

"Could I trust these two niggas?" he asked himself. He knew doing so would be taking a hell of a risk. If he allowed them to open it and view its contents, then Cash would hold him responsible if anything were to go wrong. Trap believed they were some-what trustworthy, but with 2 1/2 tickets at stake, who knows what kind of stunt these fools would try to pull.

Cash only trusted him, so to allocate that trust to two of their lowest ranking soldiers would not be such a good idea.

"Nah," he replied, making up his mind, "just do that and I got some money for y'all when y'all get back, Okay?"

They both nodded in agreement.

They knew Trap was a Made Man in the Mac, and since all of his crew was now six feet deep, they kind of figured he wouldn't trust too many people. He was no longer putting work in their hands, so to hear him say they would be getting paid to drop something off made their day.

"Alright then big homie," said Tru, giving him some dap before him and Damage walked off.

Before he pulled off, Trap sat there for a minute and watched as the two young boys, barely still teenagers, got into their Eddie Bower Expedition and pulled out of the parking lot.

He knew they were too inexperienced to handle big weight. That's why when he did hit them off with some work, it was no more than four-and-a-half ounces. A more seasoned soldier would have never asked an OG if he had wanted them to open the safe, because whatever was in it was none of their business.

Moreover, he expected that from them.

So, when they exited the restaurant's parking lot, he signaled for the black Lincoln Town Car with tinted windows, sitting across the street at the liquor store, to follow them. He'd be damned if he didn't have a backup plan for the backup plan. That was something Money had taught him a long time ago.

After putting on his Marc Jacob Aviators, he started his 2015 bumble bee painted Chevy Camaro up and pulled off. He had a long list of things to do, but the most important of them all was to get the 100 bricks he had put up in storage down to Savannah.

CHAPTER 2

THE NEW CONNECT

For the past two weeks, Peaches had been crying her eyes out. Her roommates and her teachers could not get through to her. She was always late to her classes, and her eyes would always be puffy and red. They knew something was wrong with her because she was not acting her usual self, however, she still maintained 4.0 GPA, so they figured whatever it was that had her so disheveled, it would eventually pass and allow her to continue with her life.

Life at times was too much for her to bare, and after hearing that the one man who held the keys to her heart had been killed, she'd lost hope of ever making a full recovery.

Once she realized Mercedees hadn't been to any of her classes, she began to worry all over again, calling around to try and find her. She tried calling Shay's phone too, but no one would ever pick up. Had something happened everyone and she never got word about it? She drowned in negative thoughts as the unbelievable news that Cash, and Money had both been killed. It was all over Macon how the deadly assault on the two brothers, who, with a few others, ran the underground drug trade in their city. It was not how Peaches wanted the love of her life to be remembered, and she secretly blamed herself for not intervening earlier.

As she sat in her bedroom staring at the remaining photos she had left of Cash, laying on her bed she began to weep. She would never get to feel his warm presence again. She would not have an opportunity to win him back from the THOT that stole his heart from her. No! She was only stuck with memories of disappointment. She couldn't believe how selfish she was to neglect him when he needed her most. She blamed herself for not being there to encourage him to do better and stay out of trouble. If only she'd reached out to him, maybe she could have saved him from the streets.

The last time they shared a moment together was in the club and that was a moment she would never forget. He was so handsome and domineering. The juices between her legs began to stir just from the thought of him, and despite how she would normally relieve herself from the stress of not having him, she decided to try something else.

She slid off the chair she was seated in and landed on her knees. Leaning on her bed for support she slowly closed her eyes and clasped her hands together.

"Heavenly Father..."

As she prayed, she told God everything she needed help with in order to move on and be strong. Strong for her, and strong for Cash.

***

"Cash!" Mercedees yelled, walking into his bedroom, "I need to talk to you in private, if you don't mind." She was talking to her brother but was looking at Jasmin. She didn't need a third party be in the room while she discussed something with her brother. Plus, Jasmin was starting to get on her nerves.

Every time someone needed to talk to Cash, she would get all defensive and object to him having visitors. She was really overprotective. At first, Mercedees thought it was kind of cute, but lately it had started to become ridiculous. They were perfectly safe in Richmond Hill, especially since all of their kin were nearby, so Jasmin needed to calm her nerves for a minute and allow other people to speak with him.

"It's okay baby," he assured her, letting Jasmin know that she could leave them alone for a while, "let me holla at my sister and I 'll call you when we're done, alright?"

"Okay babe," she replied, raising up out of her chair and pecking him on the lips. "I am gonna check in on the kids," but before she walked out, she gave Mercedees a long hard stare. In return, Mercedees rolled her eyes, then went and sat down next to her brother.

"Man, that girl is impossible," she started off, addressing Jasmin's obsessiveness. "What kind of golden dick did you stick in that girl to get her ass like that?" They shared a brief laugh before she continued.

"So, how are you feeling lil ugly?"

She knew it was a stupid question to ask considering the past few events that had occurred, but it was still one she needed to ask. She had been having a rough time and desperately needed someone to vent to. She'd shed as many tears as she could for her brother Money, but it was time for her to move on. A month had passed since the private funeral was held for him in their backyard, and she needed to continue on with her life. She needed to go back to Atlanta so she could finish her freshmen year at Spelman. When she was abruptly removed from class by some of Cash's men, she called the school's administration office and explained to them that she had a family emergency, and that she needed to take a week break. However, she didn't know that one week would ultimately turn into five. So now she had to talk to Cash in order to find out if it was safe or not for her to go back.

As she sat there looking at him, she was relieved by the fact that she still had at least one big brother here on earth to keep her safe. Sure, he was still recovering from the attempted assassination, but despite a few scrapes and bruises, her brother was still the powerful man she'd watched him become.

"I' m good lil ugly," he answered, trying to get a good read on his baby sister to see what was really on her mind. "My chest still a little sore though, so the doctor still got me on bed rest, but overall, I'm blessed. How 'bout you?"

"I'm okay, I guess," she replied, looking down at her nails that so desperately needed a manicure, "I' m just going through the motions and tryin' to take it a day at a time."

Cash nodded his head as if he understood. He knew his sister was strong, because him and Money had groomed her to be. He had already gotten over his brother's death and was now trying to put his plan together in order for them to get back on their feet. He just needed to hear from his little sister what was bothering her, so he could get back to strategizing.

"So, what did you want to talk to me about?" he asked, getting straight to the point.

"Well," she began, "how long do we have to be hiding out here, because you know, I got to—"

He held his hand up to silence her.

"You can go back to school whenever you are ready, lil sis."

A smile spread across her face after hearing that. It was what she wanted and needed for her to get her life back on track, leaving the past in her rearview.

"Oh my God, thank you!" she exclaimed, realizing that it was much easier than she had thought. She stood up and hugged him while he was still laid in the bed. He winced from the pain she was causing in his chest.

"Ooops, I'm sorry," she apologized, realizing she was hurting him.

"That's okay, lil ugly," he said, giving her a warm smile, " a little pain never hurt anybody."

Mercedees admired her brother for being so strong and

Positive.

"But check it out though," he continued, "I'm assigning

three of my men to watch over you while you go to school, alright?"

She looked at him reluctantly. "Bruh, I don't need three niggas trailing behind me all day while I'm at school."

"I understand that Mercedees, but shit is not safe right now, and until I know it is, that's how it's gonna be."

At first, she thought about putting up a fight, but decided to just let it go for now. He was in no condition to be arguing and getting all worried over her right now, so she submitted.

"Okay then, fine," she agreed, turning around and heading for the door.

"And lil ugly," he called after her, "nobody can know that I am alive, okay?"

"What about Peaches?" she asked, knowing how much she would love to hear that he was still alive.

"Especially her," he reiterated, putting emphasis on it, "I don't want anybody to know, okay?"

"Okay big bruh, I got you," she nodded in response. Although she wasn't into the whole street life thing, she completely understood why he didn't want to exist to the world. After all, somebody did just try to kill him.

***

It was pitch black dark outside when Trap pulled up to his cousin Tameka's trailer. She lived down a long dirt road in a double wide trailer out in East Dublin.

About a minute later, Tameka came out of the front door and sat into the passenger side seat of his Tahoe.

"What's up cuzzin'?" she said, leaning over and giving him a hug.

"Everything is gucci, Meeka," he replied, looking her over.

His cousin Tameka was as black as Midnight. Her smooth dark chocolate skin made her look like she was straight from the motherland. She also had a bright white Kool-Aid smile that captured people's attention whenever she spoke. She was far from being America's Next Top Model, but she did keep her appearance up to par. She was the type of woman that didn't attract guys by her looks, but her body had been known to cause an accident or two. The white Spanx she wore with a matching white tank top displayed her curvaceous assets and she had body for days, it was just too bad that temporarily it was off limits.

"So, what's the number on that drop?" he asked, referring to the safe that was dropped off at her house earlier that week.

"Ummmmm, if you don't smoke that right now, I'll tell you," she replied, disgusted by his attempt to fire up a blunt.

He laughed.

"Alright cuzz, you got that," he said, putting it in his ashtray. She rolled her eyes at him and said, "2.5, I think!"

"You think!" he shot back, wondering why she couldn't give

him an accurate amount.

"You heard me nigga," she replied, smiling, "cause I think you owe me big time for all that motherfuckin' counting you had me doing. Nigga, don't you know I just got through with that shit about an hour ago!"

He knew 2.5 million was a lot of money to count for one person, but that's why he waited a week to stop by there.

He gave her a slight smirk before he spoke. "Girl, I got 10 more for you in the trunk so I hope you done took a nice, good break."

She quickly turned around and looked in the back. When she saw the six black duffel bags, she looked at her cousin as if she wanted to strangle him.

"Man, come on Trap, that's way too much boo boo," she whined, thinking back to how much her hands cramped up.

He couldn't help but laugh after seeing the look on her face. "Girl, I 'm just messing with you," he joked. "Those are some of my clothes back there."

"Ugh, I hate you," she stated, playfully punching him on the arm now laughing herself from how miserable she must have looked.

"Man, you know I wouldn't do you like that."

She sucked her teeth in response, "Boy whateva!"

She looked at her cousin, proud of how far he'd came. She had witnessed firsthand how him, and his crew rose to the top. But after hearing about how all of his friends were killed, she wanted him to leave the street life alone, for good.

She had a secret crush on Money for years, so when she heard about him being killed, it hurt her deeply. She didn't know how she would've reacted if she'd gotten news that Trap had been killed as well. That probably would have broken her heart into a million pieces, and she wasn't so sure she could handle that right now.

"What's up?" he asked, noticing the look on her face as she stared at him.

"Did you think about what I said?"

He rolled his head back after he realized where this was going. "Yeah, I did," he answered, hoping that was enough to keep her off his case.

"Well?" she replied, waiting on him to continue.

"As soon as I get this shit set up in Savannah, we gone start working on that, alright!"

She had been begging him for weeks to leave the dope game alone after hearing about his friends unexpected fate. She loved Trap with all her heart and would hate to see him fall victim to the streets. He was all she had and couldn't see herself continuing on in life without him.

Ever since her baby father, Quan went to prison, Trap had been there for her and her child. He had been the only father figure her son had ever known, and her life had eventually become centered around his. Even though she didn't like his answer, she was willing to accept it for now, but the conversation was far from over.

"I hear you boy," she reluctantly replied, and then crossed her arms as she leaned on the door. "So, what do you want me to do with it?" She was back on the money.

"Put a ticket in my safe, then take 50 bands to each one of my spots. Let Mel, T, and the rest of them niggas know I said to wash them bands for me."

"What about the rest?" I'll be back to get the rest, but in the meantime, send Quan some money from my stash, and you and Jr. go out on a spree, on me."

Tameka's face lit up with joy as she thought about how she was about to go cop her a Brenna Cole handbag.

"Oh, thank you cuzz," she happily leaned over and kissed him on the lips.

He pulled back from her, shocked by the intimate response. "Girl, you a lil too happy, ain't you?"

"Boy please, you my cousin," she replied, dismissing the kiss as if it was nothing, "a little kiss ain't never hurt nobody." She then opened the passenger side door and got out, waving goodbye as she walked back towards the house. She had a shopping spree to get ready for and she'd be damned if she didn't shop her ass off.

***

"Everything is already in play loc, I'm just waiting on these cat's from "Tha Cross" to get back at me."

Trap and Cash was in the middle of discussing their plans for getting off the hundred kilos they still had. Both agreed that since Cash was supposed to be dead, it would be best to let Trap launder the money through the businesses he still owned in the Mac.

Money's entertainment company and all other assets was given over to Shay. There was a trust fund set up for her and AJ so that when he became an adult, he would inherit 50% of Money's estate. Ms. Tina and Mercedees never even thought to raise an issue over it in Probate Court, because it was Cash's orders. He had already set up bank accounts for the both of them in his will, so if anything was to happen to him, they would surely be taken care of.

Now him and his right-hand man had to strategize on how they planned on raising enough money to build an army big enough to wipe out Migo and his uncles.

Trap had already started setting up Trap houses around the Seaport so they could filter the drugs back out into the streets without raising any flags. He had a spot in a project neighborhood on the westside called Tha Cross that was moving more rocks than a dump truck. He also had four other locations that constantly pumped their product, but neither one of those were bringing in numbers like Tha Cross.

"Why?" asked Cash, not knowing to what extent Trap was talking about. "What kind of business are they bringing to the table?"

"They're tryin', from my understanding, to cop like 5 or 6 chickens apiece."

Cash shook his head.

"That's not a good idea fam," he told him. "We need every nook and cranny homie. Right now, my nigga we are not in a position to sell any weight."

"I thought we was tryin to flip this shit so we could build an army to get back at them bitch ass chicos in Texas." Trap was getting a little heated just thinking about the memories he shared with his dead homies."

Cash reached over and placed his hand on his friend's shoulder, looking him in the eyes. "My nigga, there is nothing more that I want then to drop them fools six feet deep, but we gotta be smart about this cuzz."

Trap stood up and walked over towards the window. They were in Cash's bedroom talking about their next move, and he was trying to understand what Cash was thinking.

"So, what do you suggest we do?" he asked, looking down at his deceased friend's son playing with his mother in the backyard. Cash got up and walked over to his dresser. He'd made a full recovery and was now ready to play chess. He knew in order for him to show his face again, he had to take out Manny and Negro.

After grabbing the U.S. Today newspaper from the dresser he walked over by Trap and handed it to him.

"Here, read that article," he instructed him, pointing to a picture on the front page that displayed Mexico's federal police removing numerous decapitated bodies from an 18-wheeler tracker trailer.

After quickly reading the article, he turned around with a confused look on his face. "What does this have to do with us bruh?"

Cash smiled.

"Those dead bodies that were pulled from that 18-wheeler were members of the Zeta Cartel."

After hearing Cash's explanation, he was still lost. "And?"

"And you know what," Cash started, about to reveal their new plan, "Manny and Negro are a part of the Zeta Cartel."

Trap was shocked. He looked back down at the article and said, but there was over a hundred bodies in that trailer. Who the hell bringin' the pain to them niggas like that?"

Cash smiled and said, "Our new connect, homie, that's who."

CHAPTER 3

I-95

Returning to Atlanta lifted a bunch of weight from Mercedees shoulders. The stress of not knowing how your future would turn out surely kept her nerves on edge. The bright lights and Atlanta's fast pace allowed her the opportunity to put everything that had disrupted her life, in the past.

So, now that she was back in the Peach State's Capitol, it was time to get it back cracking.

"Girl," she exclaimed, "you know damn well I was gonna make it my business to come back to the Black Mecca," she assured her friend Tiffany as they chatted over the phone.

"Well, I'm glad you're back, cause now we can go out," Tiffany stated excitingly.

Mercedees didn't like the idea of going out and partying just yet. Although she had spoken to the school officials about her making up for the lost days, she wasn't quite sure if going out was the best thing for her right now. She'd just recently lost a brother, so memories of him would constantly run through her mind throughout the day, and plus, Cash had assigned three of his thugs to watch over her. There was no telling how much information they would be reporting back to him, and she didn't want it to look like the only reason she came back was to party.

"Unh unh, girl," she began, dismissing the idea, "I can't be out-and-about, around here twerkin' and shit. My brother would kill me."

"Who?" she questionably asked, thinking both of her brothers had been killed.

"Damn!" Mercedees shook her head, realizing her mistake. "I meant my mother girl, see how fucked up I am," she cried, hoping Tiffany would buy her poor acting skills.

"Yeah girl, my bad," she replied glumly, now feeling bad herself for not considering what her friend had been through.

Mercedees knew she couldn't reveal that her brother was alive. Plus, she had three bodyguards somewhere lurking around her dormitory to ensure that she stayed safe and didn't make any foolish decisions.

"Girl, maybe next time, okay?"

"Well, alright then," Tiffany replied with defeat, "you know Darryl has been asking about you ever since you left, though."

Mercedees smiled.

"Oh yeah!" she cheerfully replied, "What has he been asking?" "The usual, where is she? When is she coming back? You know how thirsty these fools get," she laughed.

That little bit of information made Mercedees day. Darryl was a cute guy she had met at an Atlanta Hawks game when her, Tiffany, and a couple of their friends received tickets from Tiffany's brother who played for the Hawks. He wasn't a starter or even a key player, but he could get them some tickets whenever his little sister asked.

After hearing about how Darryl had been inquiring about her, she thought it would be nice to surprise him with a call.

"Girl, give me his number again." She put Tiffany on speakerphone so she could enter his number into her phone.

When she was done, she told her she would call her back later, then hung up. As soon as she did, she pressed the call button. While she waited for him to pick up she wondered if it might be time to see if he could really handle driving a luxury car as nice as hers.

***

As Trap pulled into the parking lot, he backed his truck in backwards just in case he needed to make a quick getaway. He scanned the projects to see if anybody was watching him and when he was satisfied he didn't have an audience, he grabbed the grey duffle bag off of the passenger side floorboard and got out. He knew better than to drive one of his foreign cars to the projects, so he drove his Tahoe instead. However, the 26-inch Bellagio Spinners would only allow him to be inconspicuous for so long. He knew his appearance wouldn't give him away as a dopeboy in Tha Cross, because most dopeboys from Tha Cross wore the latest urban wear like AKOO, Coogi, and LRG. Trap on the other hand was on some soft linen type apparel.

As he passed by one apartment, there was a bunch of hood rats sitting on the porch, and he heard one of the girls make a joke about what he had on.

"Girl look at this nigga here," she stated loud enough for him to hear, "he must think he P. Diddy or something." The whole porch erupted in laughter. Even Trap had a slight smirk on his face from her silly comment.

He thought to himself, "If she really knew how much money I had on, instead of crackin' jokes, she'd be chasing behind me trying to suck my dick every chance she got." It didn't matter though, because he was not into project chicks.

For now, Trap didn't give any girl the time of day. He had too much on his plate to be thinking about trying to get a piece of pussy. Their whole empire was at stake, and after hearing Cash's plan on how to get in a better position to serve Migo and his uncles the coldest dish ever, he had to play his part. Cash needed him to do what he did best, and that was trap.

He had already left the other 4 spots they had across town, where he delivered Coke and picked up cash. Savannah had been good to them lately. Matter of fact, it was so good that for every two keys of Coke he dropped off at a spot, he instructed the 90's babies who ran them to turn the two keys into three. He allowed them to take the third one and do whatever they pleased, and that was to be their pay for holding down the Trap.

He walked pass apartment after apartment and noticed how worn down the buildings were and knew that he could never go back living in such a neglected environment. Tha City, where he grew up, was a little nicer than Tha Cross, but he always went by the saying that 'if you lived in one project, you've lived in them all'. He knew there was definitely some truth to it, but he didn't plan on sticking around long enough to find out.

Knock! Knock! Knock!

Waiting on the porch he glanced around the perimeter for any unwanted attention. This was his last drop off for the day and he didn't need anything going wrong. The three little dudes he had running the trap didn't know he was coming because he never told them. That was his way of staying under the radar. He knew that if nobody knew when he was coming or going, he could avoid any unnecessary drama and keep the Jackboys off his tail.

He heard someone removing the two-by-four that was used for extra security from behind the door, so he backed up a little. When the door finally opened, they opened it just enough to give him space to walk in.

"What's good with you cuzzin," Lil Twan greeted him coming through the door.

"It's all good lil homie," Trap replied, giving Twan some dap on the way in.

When he stepped in living room, he was quite impressed. There were no excess individuals roaming around, and the apartment was real neat and clean. There was no drug paraphernalia laying around or any pistols being unnecessarily brandished. The whole place looked civilized as if a family lived there. That was a big plus in his eyes, because at every single one of the other traps he'd visited, he had to instruct the people dwelling in them not to do this and not to do that. Here, it was a completely different scenario, and because of their display of maturity, he planned on blessing them.

"Man, what y'all lil niggas in here watchin'?" he asked, walking over and sitting down next to Outcast, another one of his workers.

"Nothin much, just Shark Tank," answered Outcast, reaching over to the table and grabbing the remote. He pressed the pause button so him, Twan, and JJ could pay close attention to what Trap had to say.

Trap noticed him pause the T. V. and smiled.

"Man, I why y'all ain't got no bitches over here," he asked, not really meaning it, but trying to test them.

JJ got stood up from the loveseat and headed towards the back of the apartment saying, "Money and bitches don't mix good together on this plate big homie."

"Yeah," Twan agreed, "you can't get no money chasing these dumb ass hoes big T, but you can damn sure get hoes chasing this paper," he finished by pulling out a wad of cash.

Trap nodded in agreement because he knew they were 100 percent right. It was just so shocking how advanced these three were, when neither one of them was over the age of 19.

He remembered when him, Cash, Money, and Scrappy were all coming up in the dope game. The trappin' lifestyle for them was completely different from how these little teenagers were operating and he admired their wisdom.

When JJ came back into the room, he handed Trap a grey duffle bag identical to the one he'd came in with.

Trap, in return, gave him the one he had.

"That's a hundred," JJ informed him before returning towards the back of the apartment.

Trap nodded in response, pleased by how he didn't have to say a word about why he was there. What was understood didn't need to be explained, so he stood up and headed back over towards the door. He had already been there too long, and it was time for him to go. Before he made it to the door, though, he opened the grey duffle bag and pulled out three rolled up wads of cash.

"Hey Cast," he called Outcast, holding the money up, "are y'all still wrappin' these up in fives?" he asked, meaning five-thousand dollars.

"Yeah, why?"

"Okay then, here." He tossed two of the wad's over to Cast and handed the other one over to Twan since he was standing by to secure the door. "That's for y'all to go out tonight and have some fun. Give JJ that other five when he comes from the back, alright!"

The expression on their faces let him know he made the right decision. They deserved a bonus for playing the game the way many others should've been playing it. He was truly proud of them for their hard work, and he wanted them to know it.

"But shit," Twan began to contest, "who gone hold the trap down while we're gone?"

"Man, take the rest of the day off," he told them. "Matter of fact, I'm gonna call Mel over at the Golden Club and tell him to give y'all VIP treatment on me tonight, alright!"

JJ and Twan both gave him some dap letting him know how much they appreciated his generosity.

"Man, that's what I call real nigga shit cuzzin'," Twan thanked him. "Straight up!" he added.

Trap then opened the door and walked out, not even looking back to see if they were gonna secure it back. He knew from how they moved, it was closed and locked the minute he stepped off the porch. Those were three little hustlers he knew someday was going to be running the Seaport.

Walking pass the same porch he passed earlier with all the hood ratz on it, he heard someone shout, "Aye P. Diddy, let me get your autograph before you go!" Making the porch erupt in laughter once again. Trap couldn't help but to crack a smile as he thought to himself "yeah bitch, P. Diddy this dick in your mouth."

***

"Now son, you were doing about 88 miles per hour, so that means you were doing thirteen miles over the speed limit," Trooper Stevens informed the driver of a vehicle he had pulled over to the side of the road.

"Well," the driver stuttered nervously.

Trooper Stevens knew he had him right where he wanted him. "Yes sir, your right," he interjected, "I do want you to step out of this here fancy car you're driving."

The driver of the 2015 Lexus lowered his head in defeat. He had 50 pounds of Marijuana hid in the trunk of his car and the last thing he needed to hear right now was for him to step out of the car. He was on his way back to Mississippi from a Family Reunion in Beaumont, Texas. While down there enjoying the family functions with his kin, his cousin turned him onto a Plug for some Marijuana. So, after hearing how he could get a pound for a hundred and fifty dollars apiece, if he bought fifty, he decided to cop. As a college student, attending Mississippi State University, he knew, once he got back to campus, he could get off each one of them for at least a thousand dollars. It was a flip he didn't want to miss out on, so he quickly went to the bank and withdrew the seventy-five hundred he needed in order to cop.

However, now that a State Trooper had him pulled over, he wasn't so sure if his get rich quick scheme was really worth the risk. "Hey, son," Trooper Stevens spoke again, trying to get the guy's attention. His nervousness lead Trooper Stevens to assume he had something in his car, so he opened the car door for him in an attempt the to facilitate the process of removing him from it. "I said, I 'm going to need you to step out for me and come to the back," he continued, stepping back and placing his hand on his weapon.

The young man got out of the vehicle and walked towards the back of the car, making sure to keep his hands visible to him and the police car's dash cam. He had recently seen all over the news, how cops were killing unarmed black men throughout the U.S., and the thought of having Al Sharpton give the Eulogy at his funeral didn't quite excite him enough to resist, not even a little bit.

Walking towards the back of the cream-colored Lexus, Trooper Stevens said, "Boy, I like them shoes on your feet." He was trying to bring the tension down so he could go in for the kill.

"What are those, J's?" he asked college boy, who had a puzzled look on his face.

"Yeah—Yeah," he answered cheerfully, raising his pant leg up so the trooper could get a better look. It was the opportunity he needed to talk his way out of the situation.

Trooper Stevens looked at him and laughed, "Nah, not them son," he smiled. "Them!"

The boy looked down at where he was pointing and realized, he was talking about his 23-inch Dub rims, not the shoes on his feet. Still puzzled by the trooper's comment, the boy just smiled in return.

Beep! Beep! Beep!

"Hold on for a second champ," Trooper Stevens held up a finger to silence him while he removed his cell phone from his hip. He didn't recognize the number but knew that it was from somewhere in Georgia.

"Hello," he answered, never taking his eyes off college boy.

"Well, it's good to know you're still available when I need you old man."

Trooper Stevens didn't quite recognize the voice, but it did sound familiar. "Well, availability is still up for question," he inquired. "Who is this?"

"Oh, so now you don't remember me, huh?"

"How about you help me out, and make this as quick as possible, because I'm at work," he stated irritably.

"Man, it's your pal from the military, Mr. Lewis," Cash informed him.

He didn't believe it. He had heard that both brothers had been killed a few months ago, so how was this possible "Well," he began, not sounding convinced, "I'm going to need for you to prove that son," he replied, trying to make sure this wasn't a set up.

Cash expected this. After all, it was all over the news how him and money had been killed, so to call a few months later, professing to be a dead man did seem pretty unbelievable.

"Put it like this, Fred," he said, calling him by his first name, "I know your sons are real happy since you were able to get their college tuition paid."

'Oh my God,' Stevens thought to himself. He was speaking to a dead man. To hear that one of the Lewis boys was still alive brought a smile to his face.

"Well, well, well, Mr. Lewis," he replied, "how can I help you, sir?"

"I-95," he stated bluntly, as if that was all needed to be said. "What about it?"

"Can your influence reach that far?"

Stevens smiled after realizing where the conversation was going. He had made good money working with Cash and his brother, and so did a lot of his co-workers, but he would have to make a few phone calls first before he knew for sure whether he could provide insurance for him on I-95.

"Let me get back to you on that, alright!" he said, trying to end the call so he could get back to work.

"Say no more."

Click!

When Cash hung up, Stevens went right back to dealing

with his latest perpetrator.

"Now son, let me tell you about this problem I got," he started, turning his attention back to college boy. "Me and my wife got these two boys, right! And they want to go into the military to try and pay for college themselves, but me and the misses don't want that."

He paused to make sure the boy was paying attention. "Do you get where I am going with this story son?"

CHAPTER 4

RAYMOND

"And your name is..."

"Raymond Sanders," Cash informed the receptionist. "Okay then, let me just check right quick," she said, hitting a few keys on the keyboard before continuing. "Yes, I see it Mr. Sanders."

Cash smiled.

"We have you in room 232, upstairs on the second floor. I hope you enjoy your stay here in Miami," she finished, handing him the key card to his room.

"Thank you very much!"

Cash was traveling under the alias, Raymond Sanders, in order to stay off the radar. It seemed like everyone believed he was dead, but he wasn't trying to take any chances, especially since his plan was falling into order.

"Excuse me sir," the bellboy cut him off before he could step onto the elevator, "I'll take that for you if you want?"

"No need playboy, I got it," Cash told him, rejecting his attempt to provide customer service and possibly receive a tip. The bellboy didn't like the fact that he was of no use to Cash, but he smiled anyways to try and conceal his disappointment.

As he walked off, Cash called after him. "Say, here you go pimp," he pulled out a knot of money and handed him a twenty.

"That's for effort dawg, alright!"

The bellboy took the twenty and said, "Thanks!", continuing his way to look for another potential customer.

When the elevator doors opened, he got on and pressed the button for the second floor. The Radisson Hotel was nice and perfect for his three-day trip. He had come to Miami for business, and knew that, after leaving the city mostly known for its popular beaches, the most important part of his plan will be completed.

The only thing he was carrying with him was a brief case containing a million dollars. It was a gift he intended on giving to a future business partner, with the hopes of them helping him expand his empire.

When the doors opened for him to get off, there was a beautiful Hispanic woman standing there waiting to get onto the elevator. Before either one of them made a move to get on, or off, they stood there starring at each other for what seemed like an eternity. Gazing into her marble green eyes, he saw a woman of another breed. A woman who had class, style, and elegance; and for the first time in a long time, he thought about hollering. Just when his lips parted to speak, the elevator doors began to close, so he lunged forward with his arm outstretched to stop them from closing, and that's when she spoke.

"I am so sorry," she apologized, now stepping onto the elevator as he stood in-between the doors, allowing her to step in.

When she passed him, he quickly recognized the scent of her perfume. It was the same Chanel Bleu fragrance he'd bought for Jasmin on Valentine's Day last year. Not only did this Spanish chick smell good, but she looked even better. Her skin complexion was a smooth gold, which was probably the result of a great tan job. He knew by her heavy accent she was of Spanish descent. Her all white dress was partly laced, but in a sexy way that kept his eyes glued to her body. She had silky brown hair that stopped right below her shoulders, and exotic facial features that complemented her accent. She was a gorgeous woman, and he couldn't take his eyes off her to save his life.

"Are you getting off on this floor?" she asked smiling, wondering why he was still standing there.

"Ummmmm, yeah," he replied, snapping out of his gaze. "Sorry about that, ma," he apologized, more from embarrassment than from holding the doors.

After stepping off, he watched as the elevator doors closed, but not before she waved goodbye. He smiled in return, then turned around and that's when it hit him. He left the brief case filled with the money on the elevator.

***

"Hey mama!" Jasmin happily greeted her mother as she walked through the door.

"Hey girl," her mother replied with joy, "I'm so glad you are safe."

Ms. Myers hugged her daughter, showering her with kisses. It had been months since she'd heard from her but knew that she was alright. Trap had ordered some of his men to stop by her house once a week to check-in on her. They informed her that Jasmin was perfectly safe, however, they were not at liberty to disclose her location for security reasons.

So, when she finally got a call from her, letting her know that she was going to stop by for a visit, she hauled off to the grocery store and picked up some oxtails, Jasmin's favorite.

"Mama, what are you in here cooking?" she inquired, following her mother into the kitchen. Ms. Myers turned her head and smiled, "your favorite, 'Oxtails', they said in unison.

"Mhmmm, mmmmm, mmmm! You sure do know how to welcome a girl home don't you." She looked over her mother's shoulder as she stirred the oxtails and lima Beans around in the pot. Saliva instantly rushed to her mouth as the aroma traveled through her nostrils.

"Baby girl, why don't you go ahead and set the table up for us to eat, cause these tails is just about done."

Jasmin happily obliged, opening the cabinet that contained the plates and setting them down on the small kitchen table. When she opened the silverware draw, her mother removed the rice from the stove and placed it on the table. They sat down and said grace. Jasmin knew her mother wanted to know what was going on, and why all of a sudden she had to leave. True enough, she no longer stayed with her mother, but to leave the city without even saying goodbye was a little bit too much for Ms. Myers. Jasmin was her only child, and her best friend, so for her to lose her and be alone would devastate her.

For the most part, she was just glad to have her baby back.

"So, mom," Jasmin spoke first, digging into her food, "how has work been coming along?"

Her mother looked at her like she was crazy. She had been gone nearly 3 months without even calling or sending a letter, and here she had the nerve to ask about her job. For the past 3 months, work had been hell. She didn't know where her only child was and hadn't been convinced she would ever see her again.

"Little girl, don't you think you should be telling ME something, rather than asking me something," she suggested, placing her fork down and looking her in her eyes.

"Mom, I know I should have called, but there was—"

"Wasn't enough time to call and at least let me know you were alive," she cut Jasmin off, tears now streaming down her face.

Jasmin looked away in an attempt not to get teary eyed. She knew not calling her was going to be torture, but it was necessary. She needed to keep their location as private as possible, because not only was her life at stake, so was the love of her life.

"Oh god ma," Jasmin's voice cracked, now feeling the tears buildup in her own eyes. "I'm sorry okay, I'm sorry!"

They both looked a complete mess with tears cascading down their faces. They eventually stood up from their seats and hugged. It was the emotional release they both had been needing in order for them to move on. The past 3 months had been hell for the both of them, but now that they were putting their emotions out there on the table, their healing process could begin.

They broke from their embrace and shared a slight laugh.

"Okay, now since that is over," Ms. Myers said, ready to change the subject, "work has been work sweetheart, since you must know."

Jasmin smiled at her mother's ability to bring light to such a dark moment.

As they sat there and enjoyed their meal, Jasmin filled her in on the latest, making sure to omit a few details. The fact that she was with Cash and his family the whole time, in a safe house in Richmond Hill, didn't need to be disclosed. She told her about how Cash and his brother had been murdered, and that she just needed some time to herself to grieve. Her story was partially true, and it was going to have to do for now.

She also went on to tell her about how she was going to move to Savannah. Cash told her to tell her mother before he left for his business trip to Miami. She didn't like the idea of Jasmin moving so far away, but knowing she was safe and alive was good enough for now.

Jasmin took bite after bite of her favorite dish while they talked. The oxtails was good, but when she took in another mouthful her stomach made her take off towards the bathroom.

She vomited everything she'd just eaten into the toilet. It was a disgusting site to see, and the smell was revolting. She managed to heave up most of the rice, meat, and beans before her noticing her mother was standing behind her.

Noticing the strange look on her face, Jasmin turned around and asked, "What's wrong, Mama?"

"You're pregnant!" she replied.

***

Cash hurried down the hotel's flight of stairs as quick as he could, skipping two or three of them at a time. He felt like a complete idiot for leaving the money on the elevator. He had broken his number one rule, 'keep business first', and feared it would cost him the biggest amount ever.

A million dollars.

As he made it to the ground floor, probably breaking the hotel's previous record, he quickly scanned the lobby for the woman who had his small fortune in her possession. After unsuccessfully searching the lobby, he headed for the front door, but just when he was about to exit the building, that's when he looked over by the receptionist desk and saw her. His briefcase was sitting on the counter, and from how it appeared, they were discussing who it belonged to.

"Excuse me, ladies," he interrupted, walking up to the desk. They both turned and looked at him.

"That's him right there!" The woman on the elevator exclaimed.

"Guilty as charged," he replied smiling. He reached up and grabbed the briefcase off the counter, thankful there was still some honest people in the world.

"Please forgive me for being so clumsy," he apologized.

"No need," she insisted , we all get lost in the moment sometimes.

"Well, how about I show you my appreciation and buy you dinner tonight Ms..."

"Olivia," she stated, reaching out and shaking his hand.

"Olivia," he repeated, allowing her name to linger in the air for a moment while he took in her presence.

"And yours?" She asked, breaking the silence.

"Ummmm, Raymond," he answered, unsure about if he wanted to lie or not.

"Okay then Raymond. What time?"

"Whatever time is convenient for you." He knew he had nothing to do for the rest of the evening, so he allowed her to pick the time they were going to share a meal. He had a very important meeting in the morning, so whatever time she picked, he would be sure to end it no later than one in the morning.

"How about 7:30," she said, enjoying the comfortability of his hand still holding her's?

"7:30 it is," he agreed, breaking their embrace and the logging her number into his phone.

When they parted ways, the receptionist said to herself, "Damn, why I can't find a man like that. That was some true love at first sight type shit.

***

"Mmmmmm, booooy, you better stop," Mercedees moaned as Darryl continued hitting her from the back.

When she called him earlier and found out he would be free for the evening, she decided to let him take her out to dinner. She needed to be around someone who could bring some pleasure into her life. That pleasure turned out to be a long-lasting night of hot sex.

So, after drinking way too many Margaritas, and enjoying his interesting conversation, she was convinced that he deserved to take this Mercedees out for a test drive; and boy was he driving.

"Ssssssh," she sucked in as much air as possible as the sensation of his dick caressed the walls of her pussy. She was well overdue for some dick, and now that she was finally getting some, every nut felt like another step towards heaven.

Darryl wasn't well endowed like some of the other guys she's been with, but his six-and-a-half inches was handling business from behind. Every time she backed up onto his wood, her ass cheeks would swallow his manhood whole, clapping in appreciation of a job well done.

He was beginning to feel the momentum of his nut build up and find an exit route from his body when he pulled all the way out of Mercedees warm enclosure. The noises she was making was driving him crazy, and he knew he couldn't last much longer hitting her from the back.

"Oh my god, Darryl," she complained, rolling over onto her back, "Why did you pull out?"

She was on the verge of getting her third nut and was upset by the sudden stop.

"Baby, I'm already into you, so the more you turn me on, the lesser I am going to last," he replied honestly.

Mercedees smiled.

She knew the affect she had on him, but it pleased her to hear him say she had some knockout pussy. She enjoyed having influence over him and thought his answer was cute, just like him. She seductively bit down on her bottom lip when she noticed the sweat glistening off of his chocolate bald head. It was the same bald head she'd had between her legs a few moments ago when he was sucking on her like a lollipop. Darryl was as handsome and as boyishly cute as they come. The perspiration that covered his body made him look like a nude swimsuit model and she was ready for him to take another dip in her pool.

"Come here, boo," she instructed him, grabbing ahold of his hand and pulling him over top of her. Taking possession of his rock-hard dick and placing it back inside her causing him to groan loudly, she then took possession of his face and said, "Look at me." He was in the middle of trying not to explode when he looked down into her eyes.

She pulled his face down to her's once she knew she had his attention and slid her tongue in his mouth. They kissed, one tongue wrestling with the other while their hands caressed each other's body. They were not stroking, just enjoying the moment of being body to body. Darryl's lips eventually found their way down to one of her succulent breasts and began sucking on her nipple. He fondled the right while his mouth devoured the left. When Mercedees thought it was time for him to get back in the game, she slowly began gyrating her hips.

"Mmmmmmmm, yeah baby," she cooed, realizing the coaching and motivation made a difference, "just like that."

For the next 15 minutes, they both rode the wave as they surfed up and down his king-sized bed. Their rocky rhythm, causing the headboard to hit the wall, put emphasis on every stroke. Only passion, emotion, and hormones were being exchanged between the two as they slowly rocked each other to sleep.

***

"T P, what's good in the A? Is everything okay up there?"

TP was one of the guys Cash sent up to Atlanta to watch over his little sister. He had been standing on the roof adjacent to the building Mercedees had entered earlier when he'd gotten the call from Cash.

"Everything is cool my nigga," he informed him, letting him know that his sister was safe.

"That's what's up, fam," Cash replied, thankful she was in good hands. Make sure y'all niggas keep y'all eyes on her, okay?" TP looked over at Square who was still looking through the binoculars and shook his head.

"We definitely not gone let her out of our sight big homie," he grinned, trying to snatch the binoculars away from his homie so he could get another peek.

They had been watching Cash's little sister have sex the whole time. Not only had they seen her suck dick as good as Pinky the porn star, they watched as the bald headed guy hit her from the back.

"Okay then, y'all be easy."

Click!

"Here!" Square tossed him the binoculars and walked off.

"It's over with anyways.

TP quickly raised them up to see if he could catch a little more action, but just like his homie had said, the lights were off and the show was over.

"Damn!" He exclaimed loudly, turning around to leave as well. "Well, at least we watched her like he asked."

***

"Yes ma'am, how can I help you?" The concierge greeted Olivia as she approached his podium.

"Yes, I am supposed to be meeting someone here by the name of Sanders," she informed him.

"Oh, yes, Ms. Olivia, please follow me," the very tall and slender white man said, guiding her through the restaurant. She took in how nice and peaceful the dining area was. Every customer seemed to fit into the restaurant's harmonious atmosphere, and she knew that for her date to pick this spot to have dinner, said a lot about the kind of guy he is.

When Cash came into view, a smile spread across her face from the satisfaction of seeing him again. He was as handsome as before and was dressed to impress. Approaching the table, he stood up out of his seat and pulled out her chair out.

"Oh, thank you," she said, placing her Chanel clutch handbag on the table and taking a seat.

"The pleasure is all mines sweetheart," he replied, walking around the table to sit.

"How about I give you two a few minutes," the Concierge spoke up to let his presence be known, "and then I'll have someone come over and take your orders." He handed both of them a menu.

"Sounds good to me," Cash replied, placing the menu down in front of him.

When he walked off, Olivia spoke first, "Raymond, this is a nice restaurant."

"Yes, it is," he agreed, looking into her pretty eyes, "but nothing in here compares to how good and stunning you look."

She blushed.

"Aren't you the charmer," she replied, giving him a warm smile.

"Well, I try."

For the first couple of minutes, they complimented each other on their appearances. Cash and everyone else in the restaurant could not overlook how beautiful Olivia was. She was a gorgeous woman with a unique look. Her style and personality gave off the impression she was not green, and Cash took notice.

While they were busy enjoying their conversation, a waitress came over to take their order.

"Yes, I think I'll have the Chicken Cordon Bleu, with seasoned rice and broccoli and cheese," Olivia said, giving her order. "And you, sir," the Waitress directed her attention over to Cash.

"I'll have the same, but instead of rice, could you substitute that for steamed corn?"

"Will do," she replied, anticipating a big tip after noticing the Cartier watch around his wrist. "Will that be all?"

Cash looked at his date and they nodded in unison.

"So, Raymond," Olivia began, "what brought you to Miami?" "Business," he stated bluntly.

"Hmmmmmm, that seems to be the norm around here. Is there any other reason besides work?" She wanted to know everything there was to know about Cash.

"Well," he began, wondering if he should lie. "I'm a man all about business Olivia, so that's pretty much my reason for being down here.

"Well, that's too bad," she said, sounding a little disappointed. His eyebrows raised, "Why would you say that?"

She was really enjoying his company and was looking forward to possibly enjoying his dick entering her later on that night, so she decided to take the conversation into another direction.

She grabbed her glass of Iced Tea and used her index finger to stir the contents around in the glass. When she was done mixing her drink, she seductively sucked on her finger before continuing.

"I was sort of hoping this little business trip that you were on could possibly lead to a little pleasure."

Cash was at a loss for words. As they locked eyes from across the table, he could tell Olivia wanted to make love to him. And bad too! He didn't know how to quite respond, but he knew sleeping with her could be the worst thing he could do. Especially after everything him and Jasmin had gone through.

So, he sat there contemplating what to say, reaching onto the table and grabbing his glass of wine. Taking a sip to help ease his mind, he thought about his next choice of words. That's when his phone ranged. He knew immediately from the ringtone that it was Jasmin, so he excused himself for a minute so he could take her call.

"Excuse me for a minute, I have to take this," he told her, getting up from the table and walking off towards the front of the restaurant.

"Hey babe, how's everything going?" he answered, now standing outside.

"Everything's fine sweetheart, I just wanted to hear your voice, that's all."

That made his heart melt. Hearing her voice during an intense moment gave him goose bumps, but at that very moment, he thought about how much he loved her.

"Baby, I love you," he confessed, starting to feel a little guilty about being out on a date with someone else.

"Awwwh, I love you to babe, and I have a surprise for you when you get back."

"Oh yeah," he smiled, assuming she'd bought him something, "how much did it cost?"

She laughed at how far off he was but played along.

"Just consider what I got for you to be priceless, okay!"
"Is that right?" he said, wondering what she could have gotten him that held no value. "It sure is," she giggled.

After throwing up at her mother's house, she went out and got two pregnancy tests to see if she was right. Once she urinated on both of them, the test results were conclusive. She was definitely pregnant. It was what she wanted; and now that she was about to bring the love of her life child into this world, her life would be complete.

"Baby, can I call you back in an hour?" He asked, realizing he still had Olivia in there waiting on him.

"Well, yeah," she reluctantly replied, "why, is anything wrong?" "Nah, sweetheart, it's nothing your man can't handle" "Okay then, I'll be waiting."

"I promise not to keep you waiting long, now give me some sugar."

"Muah! I love you."

"I love you too," he stated before ending the call.

Cash started speed walking back to his table, because it was time to cut this date short. As he sat down, Olivia spoke first, "So, that was your woman or was that business?"

"My woman," he replied truthfully.

"Well, since she's not here," she reached across the table and gently stroked his hand, "how about we enjoy the rest of our evening alone in my room?"

He considered her offer to be very generous and real tempting, and knew only a fool could turn down such an offer, however, he was a fool; a fool in love.

"Olivia, I'm sorry, but that's just not gonna happen." He waived for the waitress to come over so he could pay for their dinner.

Her facial expression said it all. She was disappointed in how the date turned out. She was not the type of woman to just sleep with any man on the first date, but after being so attracted to Cash wanting to be closer to him, she'd made up her mind halfway through their date to give him a night to remember. Too bad for her, it would only be a night for her to remember.

Instead of getting upset about it, though, she decided to compliment him. "You're truly a good man Raymond."

"We'll you know what they say," he began, knowing she would understand the rest of his statement, "behind every good man, there is a good woman. So, I can't take all the credit."

Olivia smiled. She admired how he was such a gentleman, but she just couldn't allow him to get away that easy.

"Well, can we at least be friends?" She asked, hoping to at least be able to see him occasionally.

"Absolutely," he assured her, standing up from his seat. He walked around to her side and pulled her chair out.

"How about I walk you to your car and we say goodnight?" he offered with a smile.

She couldn't say no even if she tried. "I think I will have to take you up on that offer," grabbing ahold of his arm as he led the way.

CHAPTER 5

ROOM SERVICE

Boom! Boom! Boom!

"This is the police, and we have a warrant, open the door, now!

After waiting 30 seconds and hearing people scurry around on the inside of the apartment, the Chatham Narcotics Team rammed the door down.

Ba—Boom!

"Everybody get on the fucking ground!" yelled one of the CNT officers as they rushed inside.

West, who ran the traphouse for Trap, was in the middle of flushing some dope down the toilet when he heard the police in the ally attempting to ram the door down. He knew the bolt locks securing the door wouldn't hold for long, so he grabbed what dope he had with him in the back room, and ran into the bathroom.

"Open this got damn door!" He heard one of them demand as the bathroom doorknob rattled.

He still had about 3 ounces to flush, but the toilet started acting up. He looked around for another way to dispose the drugs, and that's when he noticed the drain in the tube. Just when he was about to make his move, the door bust off its hinges, knocking him into the tub headfirst. His head bounced off of the metal soap dish and left a nasty gash on the side of his head.

"Ummmmmm dummmm pulllleeesse," was all he could mumble after colliding with the soap dish.

Everything was a blur to West as the police carried him out of the apartment. The crack he had earlier was now in a evidence bag on its way to a detective's car to get processed with the rest of the other items that were confiscated from the raid.

Bags and a few of the other people who were in the Trap, were sitting down on the curb outside of the residence while one of the cops took down their personal information. They were all in the living room smoking when the police bust down the door. After detaining everyone inside, they found 2 1/2 pounds of weed, 9 ounces of crack, and 9 ounces of cocaine stashed in cereal boxes on top of the fridge. The table in the middle of the room also contained numerous items of drug paraphernalia, such as a digital scale, baggies, and a bottle of Quinine.

It wasn't the type of bust they were expecting because the anonymous tip they'd received only indicated that Marijuana was being sold out of the house. After realizing it was more than that, they contacted the Federal liaison from their department and had them come down and check it out.

"Wow, these guys were really getting it in," Agent Bradley stated, looking over the contents of the bust as they laid a across the back of a detective's car.

"Yes, they were," the detective agreed, "and I got some good news for you too," he continued cheerfully.

"Oh, yeah," the agent's eyebrow shot up from interest, "whatcha got detective?"

The detective turned around and pointed to the curb where everyone was seated in hand cuffs. "That young man said that he was willing to cooperate."

Agent Bradley couldn't believe her ears. To have someone cooperate so early in the investigation was a major step for her, because usually she would have to engage in a long intense interrogation where she tried to turn a so-called Real Nigga into a snitch.

As she walked over towards the young man who would be her rat for the next couple of months, she pulled out her notepad and prepared to take notes.

Bags, looked up when he saw the black lady in the dark grey pants and white button up shirt walk over to him. She wore a badge around her neck that displayed the emblem of a federal agent. As she approached him, he shook his head because he knew things had just gotten worse.

"So, Bags," she greeted him by his street name, smiling as she towered over him, "I heard you wanted to speak with me."

***

Cash woke up at the sound of someone knocking on his room door. His cell phone was cradling his face, so he removed it from between him and the pillow. He was still fully clothed and remembered talking to Jasmin last night. Obviously, their conversation put him to sleep, so he planned on calling her back before heading off to his meeting.

Knock! Knock! Knock!

"Room Service!"

Hearing the hotel staff knocking, he got up to answer the door. "No thank you," he said, looking out the peep hole. He saw a Hispanic man standing there with a food cart.

"Senor, this is your free complimentary breakfast," the staff member announced, as if Cash had won the lottery.

Cash figured it wouldn't hurt to eat some breakfast while he waited for Jose to come and get him for his meeting. So, he opened the door and allowed the short Spanish dude to wheel the cart into the room.

"Good morning, Senor," the vibrant Mexican greeted him

as he pushed the food cart past him into the middle of the room. Cash was still trying to wake up, so he barely pushed the door closed as he tried to focus in on the Mexican.

"So," he began, walking over to see what this free breakfast was all about, "what kind of free—" he stopped mid-sentence when he noticed the Mexican turn around with a Desert Eagle in his hand with a silencer attached to it. Shocked by the sudden change of events he quickly contemplated his next move, but before he could do anything, two sets of hands grabbed him from behind. As he attempted to turn his head and see who it was, a dark colored bag was placed over his head.

"Don't resist amigo, or we will kill you right here," he heard one of them say before they escorted him outside the room.

***

"What's good, Mr. Porter?" Bryan cheerfully greeted Trap, walking into his office and taking a seat in the chair intended for his clients. "Can I help you with anything?"

Bryan didn't like the fact that Trap had been in his office on his computer while he was out having lunch. It wasn't proper business etiquette to just pop up on your business partner and start rumbling through their files. Although he believed Trap was being very disrespectful, he did appreciate him finally wearing some casual clothes to their establishment instead of the urban wear he usually wore.

"Bryan," Trap called out to him, looking up from the computer. "Where is the fifty-grand my assistant brought over here for you to wash?" He looked into Bryans eyes as he nervously fidgeted in his seat.

"What do you mean?" He asked, getting up and walking around the cherry oak desk.

Trap eyed him suspiciously as he came and stood behind him. His bony 6-foot frame towered over Trap while he remained seated. He adjusted the Polo frames on his long face so he could look at what he was referring to.

Although, he looked young and inexperienced, Bryan was skilled at what he did. A graduate of Georgetown, Bryan could fool a lot of people with his innocent appearance. However, Trap was no sucker, and he made it his business to slide in on his business partner periodically to make sure he was managing their business appropriately.

Trap met Brian about a year-and-a-half ago when he was helping Money find talent for his entertainment company, To Be Determined. He became Money's accountant after helping them wash the illegal drug money they had been acquiring through the company. He was responsible for making sure that every dollar made appeared to be funds made from the business.

Now that Money's company had been dissolved and liquidated for Shay and AJ to live comfortable, Trap decided to keep him on their team. He knew Bryan was good at what he did, so he hired him to oversee the Armani Foundation.

The Armani Foundation was a non—profit Organization set up for displace mothers and children who had become victims of the urban community, particularly, when fathers were either murdered or incarcerated for a long period of time, the foundation would swoop in and support the family financially, emotionally, and mentally, until they could get back on their feet. Cash thought it would be a nice thing to do in remembrance of his brother.

However, as Trap perused through the different accounts set up in the QuickBooks software, he noticed that only forty thousand had been slowly incorporated into the business account. From what he could see, ten thousand was donated once a week from private donors in a month's time. That explained what transactions had taken place, but that wasn't the problem. The problem was, the last transaction that took place was almost three weeks ago, and there was no final deposit anywhere after that to explain where the other ten grand went.

"Let me see what we got here," stated Bryan, bending down to take a look at the accounts. He knew the money wasn't on there, but he hoped to God he could convince Trap there was an error somewhere in the account to get the attention off him.

Trap stood up from Bryan's chair and walked over to the door to make sure it was locked. He didn't need anybody walking in on them while he discussed business with his partner.

Bryan knew it wasn't a good sign when he noticed him lock the door. He was terrified of Trap and didn't want to have any misunderstandings with him about money.

"Bryan," Trap called him in his most serious tone.

]

"Yea- yeah, I- I'm looking for it now Mr. Porter. He was stuttering like the boxer from the movie Harlem Nights.

"If you sit up here and lie to me," Trap warned, heading back over to where Bryan was seated, with a gun now in his hands.

Bryan had an erratic look on his face. His knees were jumping all over the place as he remained seated, glancing back-and- forth between the black handgun in Traps hand and the computer screen. What scared him the most, was that Trap was very calm.

As he approached Bryan, he began maneuvering his chair farther away from Trap, so if he got the chance, he could get up and make a run for it.

Too bad for him, Trap peeped the move.

"If you move your chair any farther, my nigga," Trap paused for a minute to raise his Glock to his head, and then said, "I will make your wife and kid a recipient of this organization. "Do you understand me?"

Bryan was so scared, he just nodded in return.

Trap walked over to him and grabbed him by his tie, lifting him up so he could look him in the eyes.

"Now, where is it you thief?"

"I lost it gambling," he blurted out on the brink of passing out. He hoped and prayed, by him confessing, Trap would show him some mercy.

He pushed Bryan back down into his seat and placed the gun back onto his hip. "Now, was that so hard?" He asked, walking back around the desk and sitting down.

Bryan couldn't believe it. Trap appeared relieved he finally told him the truth. If he knew he would've taken it so well, he would have been honest from the jump. For a minute though, he stayed seated, because he wasn't sure what was going to happen next.

Trap's phone began ringing, so he answered it, "Hello."

That was Bryan's cue to slide back up to his desk, but not without noticing Trap's eyes follow him as he talked on the phone.

"Okay, good lookin' out dawg," he spoke into the phone, "I'll be back down there tomorrow, alright?" Trap nodded his head and then hung up.

"Mr. Porter, I-"

Trap put his hand up to silence him.

"Yes Bryan, you are a thieving ass piece of shit!"

Bryan nodded in agreement.

"But," Trap stood up and walked towards the door, "I know people make mistakes, so I am gonna let you make this right." He was all ears.

"The next time you get paid, make sure you donate fifteen thousand to my homie's foundation, okay!"

Bryan wanted to contest, but he knew he was dead wrong and should be thankful for his life. After all the stuff he'd heard about Trap and their empire, he didn't want to have any bad blood with any member of their crew.

"And Bryan," Trap called, catching his attention before leaving, "let's not make this mistake again."

And then he was gone.

CHAPTER 6

CONTROL BUY

For hours, Cash remained seated next to two people he assumed were Mexicans. Although they hadn't spoken a word since they kidnapped him he figured they were some members of Manny and Negro's Cartel. He was still in disbelief as to how they had found him. There were so many things running through his mind, it was becoming hard for him to think straight.

Somewhere along the way of this trip, somebody in the vehicle must have felt threatened by his presence, because they placed zip ties around his wrist. He knew from that point, whatever was going to take place, it was going to be out of his control.

All of a sudden he felt the vehicle come to a halt. The person seated on the left had gotten out and began pulling him from the vehicle. The scent of forestry, and the lack of city noise led him to assume that he was somewhere in a wooded area.

"Camina!" Ordered one of the Mexicans before he felt a gentle push forward.

Cash didn't know where he was going but wasn't sure if he was about to step off a cliff or not. He heard people moving around him, but they maintained the same silence they held when they were in the car. Just when he was about to give up wondering what was going on, somebody placed their hand to his chest, stopping him from going any farther. The black bag was snatched from his head, and for a minute, he had to adjust his eyes so he could see clearly.

"What's up Cash?"

As his vision became clearer, he noticed that the man in front of him, speaking to him, was no one other than Jose.

"Sorry about the kidnapping fool, but you know it was necessary right?" asked Jose, making sure Cash didn't feel any animosity towards him.

Cash nodded.

When Jose stepped out of the way, two men approached him. They were both short Mexicans, but very clean cut. The one on the left had on what appeared to be a black tailor-made suit with matching dress shoes and a colorful tie. His hair was slicked to the back, obviously the result of some good gel, and his skin complexion was probably the lightest out of them all.

The Mexican on the right, had on some khaki pants and a Polo shirt. The Polo logo on his short-sleeved collar shirt matched the color of his Mauri Gators. He sported a fade and wore some Marc Jacob Aviators to conceal his eyes. Cash secretly admired his sense of fashion, because he had never seen a Mexican dress as good as this one.

"So," the Mexican with the Polo shirt spoke first, "you wanted to speak with me, so what do you want?" He took off his Aviators and gave Cash a long hard stare.

This was the moment he had been waiting for. The only reason he was in Florida in the first place. He didn't expect to be welcomed with open arms, but knew what it would take for him to see this man. Jose had assured him that he could make it happen, so as he stood in front of the notorious drug lord, Felix "El Fantasma", or "The Ghost", Fortunado, he smiled.

Moments ago he thought he was heading to an early grave, but as it turned out, he was meeting the leader of the Soto Cartel.

***

"I'm gonna need for you to speak into the mic so we can make sure it's working properly," Agent Bradley told Bags, while another agent adjusted the wire on the inside of his coat.

"Now, repeat after me," she instructed, before counting, "1, 2, 3, 9, 4..."

"Good!" she said, giving him a thumbs up.

"Now, make sure you get him to say something about the drugs so we can get a warrant for this guy."

"But he's not even that type of dude," Bags tried convincing her, "I barely even speak to him, so it's gonna be—"

"For your sake, he better say something," she fiercely cut him off. She didn't have time to play games with him. The low-level drug pushers he was trying to set up was not good enough for her. She wanted the person who supplied them with the cocaine and was responsible for distributing drugs in her city. As a veteran agent, she wasn't into frying the little fish that roamed the Seaport streets where she grew up. She was looking forward to prosecuting the big ones. She had a personal vendetta against the drug trade and everyone who distributed its products.

It all started in high school, but her brother, Michael, was in college at Georgia Southern. He was just about to finish his senior year and start his career in managing corporate businesses when he was arrested for simple possession of Marijuana right around the corner from campus. It was not the kind of charge he wanted on his record when he got the chance to submit his resume to anyone of the Fortune 500 Companies, he planned n working for. After hearing from the police how much time he was facing for the felony charges, he panicked. His whole career was about to go down the drain, all because he wanted to smoke with a few of his frat brothers.

However, the cops who arrested him were part of a local narcotics team that recruited individuals for making drug buys from the local dealers. They offered him a chance at having his charge dismissed if he executed three controlled buys. At first, he rejected, because he knew his life would be in danger, but after constantly being badgered and reminded that his chance of having a wonderful career could be snatched away, he gave in.

The first two buys went smoothly, but on the third something went terribly wrong. The team members who were supposed to surveillance him, lost contact with him when the dealer, at the last moment, changed the location of where they were supposed to meet. The Police didn't discover the body until the following week, when some local fishermen found him naked by the riverbank with a rat stuffed into his mouth. The story made headline news, and when his little sister, Veronica, got the update on her cell phone about the discovery of her sibling, she lost it. She stayed in a state of depression for almost a year, until she vowed to avenge her brother's death.

Now, if Bags thought she would let him just bring her anybody, he was sadly mistaken.

"I don't have time to play games with you Bags," she spoke with authority, putting emphasis on his name, "so, are you going to fully cooperate with me, or do I need to contact the U.S. Attorney's Office and have them proceed with an indictment as long as Abercorn Street?"

Bags felt totally defeated. He realized at that moment he'd made a deal with the devil. He took off his Georgia Bull Dog hat and wiped the sweat from his brow. Although the temperature in the van was pretty cool, he was sweating like a runaway slave. Agent Bradley had the full court press on his ass, and he was looking for someone to pass the ball to.

"No," he finally mumbled, "I'll do whatever you need me to do."

"That's what I thought," she snapped, wanting to add 'bitch' to the end of her statement, but kept it professional.

"Alright, Agent Graham!" she shouted towards the front of the van.

They pulled off from the federal building and headed to the location he planned on meeting Trap. Agent Bradley smiled at the thought of getting another one of the people responsible for her brother's death off the streets. As she looked towards the sky, she hoped that he was looking down on her, pleased with her effort.

***

Mercedees was tired of sitting in class listening to the boring ass professor give a speech about U.S. Politics. She knew all about the crookedness of the U.S. Government and what its elected officials had to offer. However, Political Science was one of the courses mandated in her curriculum in order for her to get her degree.

"Okay, students," said the old white man standing next to the projector, "make sure you read chapter 16 and 17 this weekend, and I'll see you..."

The students were already exiting the building before he even got a chance to tell them bye. It was the weekend, and this was Mercedees final class of the week. She couldn't believe how difficult some of her class work was, and doubted if she would have any time to party. All of her professors wanted her to read at least two chapters out of the huge textbooks she purchased from the bookstore. College was beginning to seem not so fun after all, that is, until she got around the local boys from Atlanta.

Making her way out of the Jefferson Building, she wondered why everyone seemed happy. She didn't know if it was the weekend that had everyone so cheerful, or if everyone had big plans while she studied. According to Peaches, she claimed to have suffered the same kind of boredom and disconnection her freshmen year at Spelman. At first, it was all about getting good grades and staying on top of her schoolwork, but then, after completing her junior year, her future began to look more dubious. One day, she would be having a conversation with a post-grad coordinator about securing her a job at a law firm once she graduated. Then next, she would be filling out applications to enroll in the numerous law schools that would help her further her career.

Mercedees didn't see herself having those types of problems. She knew exactly what she wanted to do. She just had to remember her mission and complete her goals.

As she continued on across campus, her intuition kept eating at her. Something was telling her that someone was watching her. For a minute, she thought about taking a detour towards Packard Hall, but then she remembered the three bodyguards sent to tail her. When she finally made it to her building, she turned around looking for her three Kevin Costner's, but couldn't see them. That's when she came up with an idea.

She walked over to the nearest bench closest to the front of her building and sat her bag down. After quickly glancing around to make sure nobody was looking, she slowly began unbuttoning her red Stacey Holmes polyester blouse. Taking her time, she gently caressed her c-cup breast as her Victoria Secret bra slowly became exposed. She began swaying her hips from side to side as her tongue slithered across her top lip. She was beginning to enjoy being a seductress, closing her eyes as she imagined how it would feel to have sex outside.

"Girl, what the hell is wrong with you?" asked Peaches, standing there with two of her classmates, shocked.

"Oh my god!" Mercedees gasped, embarrassed by her seductive display. She quickly turned away from them and began buttoning up her shirt, "How long have y'all been standing there?"

"Girl, long enough," laughed one of the girls.

Mercedees felt stupid for even trying to do something fun. The girls were laughing at her, and Peaches tried hard not to laugh, but it was infectious.

"Girl, are you okay?" she asked her, trying to hold back her laughter.

Once she got her shirt buttoned, she grabbed her book bag and stormed off. She'll be damned if she became the laughingstock for the weekend. Although she was still embarrassed about being caught, on the way into building she smiled to herself at how silly she could be.

***

"Man, come on!" T P, Square, and Juvi all shouted from inside the Tahoe as they witnessed Mercedees getting caught. All three of them had seen when she exited the Jefferson building, heading off towards her dormitory. Juvi, who was in the driver seat, slowly tailed behind her as she walked. They were trying their best to watch over her and keep her safe, but she was starting to turn her three bodyguards into secret admirers.

"Man, ain't no tellin' what the fuck, she was about to do next cuzz," TP complained, disappointed he didn't get to see some more action.

"I'm tellin' you," Square agreed from the back seat. They all placed their binoculars on their lap and sat back in their seats. After hearing from TP and Square what he missed the other night on the roof, Juvi made it business to go out and get 2 more binoculars that was fully equipped with night vision and all the other special features. He had missed the episode when she was having sex with Darryl in his apartment and vowed never to miss another one. As he put the car in park, he looked at his homeboys, who were obviously still getting over the fact they wouldn't see her go any further, and said, "Man, I think I'm in love." TP and Square both looked at him and bust out laughing.

CHAPTER 7

BAGS

Trap had a lot on his mind lately. Tameka had been blowing his phone up asking if he'd made up his mind yet about leaving the dope game, but he didn't know what to tell her. He knew she could never understand the position he was in. He had to ride this thing out with Cash before he even considered turning in his G-Card. Too much blood had been shed, and there was too much money was at stake. He was going to continue holding his best friend down no matter what. There was no other option for him at this point, and he knew it.

The fact that Bryan was stealing from them left him perturbed. He never would have thought, Bryan, out of all people, would have a gambling problem. It was that kind of disloyalty that kept him by his homie side. He knew Cash needed a real friend to watch over his affairs, so he made it his personal business to stay on top of each and every single one of their businesses. No one was going to mess their plans up and hinder them from getting what they rightly deserved, and that was revenge.

Now, he just had to fix this one little problem he had with one of his Trap houses getting raided.

He had received a call from the dude Bags earlier in the week about what transpired, but made sure the conversation was as discreet as possible.

"Yeah, what up Bags?" Trap answered the phone.

"Shit, chillin' big homie," he replied. "I was just hittin' you up to let you know I was at home."

Trap knew something was wrong, because if he wasn't at the Trap working, then something was not right.

"Oh yeah," Trap pondered on the idea of what could be going on. "What you watchin' over there at the crib?

That was the signal for Bags to explain what happened. "Cops!" He stated bluntly.

Trap shook his head at the bad news. His trap in The Village had been compromised. He had to return back to Savannah and find out what had taken place, and why was Bags calling him instead of West. He figured West must have gotten locked up, but wondered why Bags was still free. He left West in charge of the Trap, so there was a possibility Bags could've gotten away if West took all the heat. Either way, he knew how to deal with the situation without exposing himself too much. He told Bags to meet him Saturday, downtown by the River Walk. He knew he was taking a chance meeting him there in the open, but if things got out of hand, he was going to make a quick exit into the crowd of pedestrians that normally flooded that area.

***

Making his way down the steps towards the River Walk, Trap saw Bags leaning on a rail watching people walk by. He glanced around to see if anybody was watching him but didn't see anyone nearby looking suspicious. He knew the Feds worked in mysterious ways, but so did he.

When Bags saw him coming his way, he walked over to the nearest bench and sat down. He was hoping he could stay seated so Trap wouldn't notice his leg shaking. He didn't know too much about him, but what he did know was that Trap was an out-of-towner who came and blessed his homeboy with some work. West said he had met Trap when he was in the "A" promoting his CD. They exchanged numbers after Trap informed him about Money's entertainment company, suggesting he could possibly help him out with getting exposure. From there, they stayed in touch, and when

Cash discussed the move with him to relocate, he kept West in mind as an asset.

"What's going on with you, family?" Trap walked up and gave him some dap.

"Same ole shit, big homie, that's all," replied Bags still seated, observing Trap size him up.

"So, what's the deal?" Trap placed his foot up on the bench so he could lean on his knee while he watched the birds fly over the river.

"Where's my lil partner West at? I haven't heard from the kid in a minute."

"Well," Bags swallowed hard before he continued, "he's locked up."

Trap looked at him for a few seconds before he replied, which made Bags feel even more uncomfortable.

"Is that so," he stated skeptically. "I guess I won't be seeing him for a while then, huh?" He looked off as if he was in deep thought, he was trying to get a good read on the dude Bags, but he couldn't quite figure him out yet. Since West was locked up, he wasn't sure if he wanted to continue doing business with Bags. After all, he barely even knew the kid.

"Listen big homie," Bags began, standing up so he could look Trap in his eyes, "how about you make me your lil partner?" Trap eyed him suspiciously.

"What if I can do the same thing West was doing, but quicker?" He was in full acting mode now. He had confidence in his demeanor and was no longer nervous. For a slight minute, he had forgotten he was wearing a wire.

Trap nodded his head in response.

"I'll tell you what," he pondered, removing his foot from the bench and standing up straight, "how about you meet me later on at the Golden Club and we'll talk about it then, okay."

Bags smiled.

"Now, that's what's up cuzzin." He shook Trap's hand as they embraced, then turned around and walked off.

Trap stood there for a minute until he was completely gone from his sight, then he pulled out his Galaxy 6S and dialed a number.

***

"Yeah," Damage answered on the first ring.

"Yo, how much time you got left?" Asked Trap.

"Ummmm," he looked over at Tru, who was operating the Drone and asked, "how much time you got left in the air cuzz?" "2 hours and fifteen minutes," he replied.

"About 2 hours my nigga," he informed him, not mentioning the fifteen, because that was going to used to land.

"Alright, then, keep y'all eyes on that nigga for me cuzz and

let me know where he goes from here."

"Will do, OG."

Then, they ended the call.

Damage and Tru had been sitting in the Expedition watching Trap's meeting with Bags. He called them right after he'd gotten the call from Bags, and knew exactly what to do in order for him to find out the truth. Then on top of that, he sent a lawyer down to the Chatham County Jail to put money on West's account and find out what was really going on. It's not that he didn't trust Bags, because he didn't trust anybody. It was basically to make sure that all T's were crossed, and all i's were dotted before he went any further. There was no room for any error or mistakes to be made. One slip could send them all to a grave, or a cell, and he wasn't trying to see either one.

If Bags story checked out, and he had in fact slipped through the Judicial System's cracks, then Trap would have no problem recruiting him.

He needed loyal men who knew the Seaport to sell his product, however, if Bags was up to something else, and was playing games, Trap would make him an example of the game he should have never claimed to know how to play.

***

After running everything down to his kidnappers, Cash was hoping his vision for developing a major distribution network could be seen through the eyes of the men before him. He had laid it all out on the table for Felix about what his intentions were. All except the part where he planned on using their resources to wipe out the Zeta Cartel. He assumed that would be the icing on the cake once he gained their trust, because technically, they had a common enemy.

"So, you mean to tell me," Felix began, trying to get a full understanding of what Cash was proposing, "is that you can put together an operation that will guarantee us distribution of up to a thousand kilos of cocaine in one month, and all we have to do is get it to the States?"

Cash nodded with confidence.

Felix seemed to ponder the idea for a long time as he walked back and forth in front of Cash. His hands were clasped behind his back as he paced like a distinguished gentleman. The information he'd just received was phenomenal and quite questionable. He had never heard of Cash, and the mere fact that he was professing to have the capability of moving more dope than any other distributor in his organization was remarkable.

As he stopped walking, he snapped his finger and beckoned for his other comrade, the one with the tailor-made suit, to approach him. Cash watched them whisper back and forth to each other. That was an indication to him, Felix was smarter than Manny, because when he first met Manny and his brother Negro, they made the mistake of assuming he didn't speak Spanish. Felix, on the other hand, didn't even take a chance on speaking his native language and having it understood by an outsider. He played it smart and safe, and Cash's level of admiration was raised a little higher for the so-called Ghost.

When they ended their side conversation, Felix walked back over to face him and said, "This gift you have for me, where is it?" He asked suspiciously.

"It's in my hotel room in—"

Felix put his hand up to silence him. He snapped his fingers towards one of the men behind Cash, and before anything else was said, the briefcase was brought in front of them.

"Is this the gift you have for me?" Felix asked sternly.

"Yes, the combination is 06—16—85."

Jose took the briefcase away from the henchman and entered the combination. He opened it up and turned it around so Felix could view its contents.

After two seconds, he surprisingly looked back at Cash and said, "How much is this?"

"A Million Dollars," he answered seriously.

Felix's whole demeanor changed once he realized what Cash had to offer. It was a symbol of respect, and he knew it. You just don't send word through a cartel member that you want to meet the leader of that cartel. That was just not how things were done, but when Jose, his wife's nephew, contacted him and told him about Cash, he took it upon himself to see what this local drug dealer had to say.

Felix closed the briefcase and waved for Jose to take it away. Stepping closer to Cash, he stared into his eyes and said, "I had plans on killing you today my friend for wasting my time."

Cash broke a sweat.

"When Jose brought this to my attention, I thought it was a joke." He paused to look at Jose, then back at Cash, "But I've come to realize that you are no good to me dead, and clearly, this is no joke," he ended with a slight laugh.

He stepped back some and ordered for one of his men to cut the zip tie off of his wrist. "Let's walk and talk," he told Cash, leading the way, "so, I can hear more about this elaborate plan you have."

***

"I would like to thank all y'all pimps, playas, and macs for coming out tonight and representin' that Seaport," the DJ announced over the Golden Club's Bose speakers. "We got some of the baddest ladies this side of the country has to offer, so y'all get them check books out, throw them bands, and put them EBT cards away, cause we about to turn up in this bitch!"

The Golden Club was everything its name claimed it to be. There were painted gold walls all over the place, gold bottles being passed across the glass bar, and beautiful naked women with golden tans, sashaying around the club looking for their next trick. It was an environment for those who was either trying to spend it all, or lose it all.

However, Trap wasn't there for that. He had business to tend to. As he sat in his private booth in the corner away from everyone, he thought about everything that had taken place lately. Too many events were occurring back-to-back. But, on the flip side, he heard from Cash and found out that the meeting with the notorious Ghost went well. He was wondering why he hadn't heard from him and was about to send some guys down there to find him, but then he finally called.

Now, since that was out of the way, he had one more matter to deal with.

"How you doing, baby boy?" Big Mel walked up and greeted him.

Trap stood up to embrace his partner. "Everything's well dawg, how's the wife and kids?" he asked sincerely.

"They're good, they're good!" He replied with a slight nod.

Big Mel was the owner of the luxurious Golden Club, and a longtime friend of Trap's. When Cash came home with the connect from Texas, and they blew up, he invested a lot his money into various businesses across Macon. He had barbershops, car detail shops, and a bunch of other business ventures looming across Bibb County. One in particular business he had on his radar was a local strip club called Shakers. It was one of the few in the city that was barely getting by at the time, and Mel, the owner, was up to his knees in debt over the club's overdue bills. He desperately needed someone to bail him out, so that's how Trap came in the picture.

Mel noticed him when Trap and a few members of his crew came into the club one night and threw thousands of dollars as if it was nothing but Monopoly money. It was the opportunity he had been looking for. So, before the night was over, he pulled him to the side and introduced himself. He thanked him for stopping by and supporting his establishment, then he gave him his business card and told him to call first thing in the morning. Trap gave him his word he would, and he did. From there, they discussed a deal on a temporary partnership, where, if Trap helped finance the relocating of his club, Mel would pay him back double his money in 2 years and allow him free membership into the club for as long as it existed. Trap thought it was a great idea and put the money behind him.

Once the Golden Club was up and running, it instantly became a success, attracting people from all over South Carolina, Georgia, and northern parts of Florida. He recruited some of the finest women around, putting them in an environment that would bring plenty tricks, dope boys, and hustlers their way.

Mel leaned close to his ear and said, "Everything's in motion for you big dawg, alright!" he informed Trap, patting him on the shoulder before walking off.

Trap nodded in return and sat back down. All he needed now was for Bags to show up.

***

Ten minutes later, he saw Bags walk through the front entrance. He watched him peek around, obviously looking for someone, so Trap held his arm up until he could see where he was seated.

When he walked over, they embraced for a moment, giving each other dap before sitting down in the booth. Bags could tell that Trap's mind was not on any of the women in the club, because when he sat down, he got straight to the business.

"Now listen," he leaned over to Bags so he could whisper, "I'm gonna bless you just like I blessed West, but I am gonna need for you to find another location for us to set up shop, ya feel me?"

Bags nodded in agreement, then whispered back, "How about we discuss this outside my nigga, cause this music in here is loud as fuck." He knew with the music blasting, the wire behind his chain would not pick up what was being said.

Trap didn't like the idea of leaving the club to discuss business, especially since that was the very reason, he picked the inside in the first place. He knew Bags wasn't playing it fair, and he wasn't about to get him jammed up.

After their meeting down by the riverwalk, he had gotten a call from the lawyer he'd sent down to the jail to see West. He informed Trap that West told him Bags was cooperating with the Feds. Then, when Damage contacted him and said they watched him leave the meeting and hop in the back of what appeared to be a dark colored Astro Van, it confirmed everything. All the evidence pointed towards Bags being a Federal Informant, and Trap was not going to allow him the opportunity to set him up.

"How about this pimp," he began, talking loud enough for the wire to hear him, "let's just enjoy the ladies for a moment and we'll chop it up later, okay?" He waved for one of the waitresses to come over to their table.

"Hey, handsome, what can I get for you fellas," asked the dark-skinned waitress, showing off her half naked curvaceous body.

"Let us get that Gold Bottle special sweetheart!" he shouted over the music, placing 5-hundred-dollar bills on her tray.

She smiled at his generous tip, then hurried off to go get their bottles of Champagne.

"Say Big T," Bags called over to him, "all this is not necessary big homie, and I appreciate the love-" he stopped after seeing the serious expression on Trap's face. He knew he was being disrespectful declining his generosity, but he was trying to hurry up and fulfill his end of the bargain. He didn't feel comfortable being around Trap any longer than he had to.

When the waitress came back with their bottles, she brought 3 strippers along to keep her customers entertained. Two of them started entertaining Bags, while the third sat on Trap's lap. After opening their bottles and filling both glasses, she handed one to Trap, and one to Bags. She watched Bags guzzle his down and focus back in on his entertainment.

Trap watched as Bags popped one of the strippers tits in his mouth and sucking on its nipple. He knew from that point on, this would be a night to remember.

CHAPTER 8

FBI

"Checkmate!" Trap declared, taking his queen and locking him in a corner.

For a few seconds, Cash was in denial as he surveyed the board for another way out. It was Trap's third time winning, ending their best out of 5 series, and Cash didn't like that.

"It's over dawg," Trap smiled, leaning back in his chair and locking his fingers behind his head. "Now let me hear our moniker, my nigga."

Cash looked up from the board and laughed.

"Okay brain, you got that."

"That's right, I do..." Trap leaned forward with his hand to his ear, waiting on Cash to complete his sentence. "Pinnnnkey," he mumbled getting up from his chair and walking over to the liquor bar to fix them a drink.

"Excuse me!" Trap got up and followed him so he could hear him repeat it more clearly.

"Pinky, nigga!" Cash stated clearly, "I am Pinky, got damn!"

They both shared a slight laugh as Cash passed him his drink. They were downstairs in the living room of Cash's mansion discussing the latest developments when he grabbed the chessboard. He found a liking to the strategic game in prison, where he would often engage in fierce battles with

Migo. Migo was a pretty good player too, but he turned out to be an even better coach. For a while, he would beat Cash senseless, sending him to his cell on numerous occasions wearing a latex glove. That was an indication to everyone around the unit that he had loss 5 games in a row. After hearing so many comments and jokes about wearing it, he made sure to tighten his game up and start returning the favor. So, for about 2 months straight he read books written by some of the best chess players around the globe. He learned to take his time moving his pieces and never leave a piece unprotected meaning. The art of thinking 5 to 8 steps ahead of your opponent came natural after that, so he didn't need any more help.

Anyways, after doing some homework and long nights of practice, he eventually became better at the game and started making Migo wear the glove instead. Now that he was out, the idea of wearing a glove was too ridiculous for him to wager. So, him and Trap came up with the idea that whoever won, he would have the benefit of being Brain for the day, while the loser answered to his sidekick's name, Pinky.

"Hey, Pinky," Trap called him. He was standing by the sliding glass door that led to the side of the house. "Let's go outside for a minute, because I have to tell you about the other night."

Cash already knew what he was referring too.

When Trap arrived at his house earlier, he tried informing him about the rat that tried to infiltrate their organization, but Cash told him to hold off discussing it, because the girls were still around and he never wanted them to know any details about their business.

Now that they had time to talk, he followed him out the door and onto the concrete patio. Cash led the way as they walked through a maze filled with bicycles and four-wheelers.

He stopped when they reached the outdoor jacuzzi, sitting down on one of the ledges and gesturing for Trap to do the same. After taking a seat, he ran down everything that had occurred between the time Bags called him, and the night at the Golden Club. He knew Cash shared his level of tolerance when it came to snitching, so he knew he would be pleased. At first, Cash was shocked, stating, "Why didn't you kill him?"

Trap knew that would cause too much unnecessary attention. He knew if he killed Bags that night, the Feds would not stop until they had everyone behind bars.

"My nigga, I'm positive by the time he left the club, he was in a completely different world. The waitress kept bringin' him laced drinks, and he kept knockin' them bitches back."

Cash nodded, agreeing with his decision.

"Listen," he continued, laughing as he thought back to that night, "before I left that idiot in the club, the girls had done took all that fools money, and made him eat their pussy like it was the last supper."

Cash laughed.

Trap enjoyed telling the story, because once Bags finally left the club, the idea of him setting someone up was no longer an issue. He was going to be stuck in la-la-land for the rest of his life, and no matter how much Agent Bradley would try to sober him up, Bags would never be the same.

***

"That son of a bitch!" Agent Bradley grimaced on her way out of the hospital.

She had been in the psychiatric ward all day trying to find out why her informant was acting like a child. His thought process was off balance, and he couldn't explain why he stayed in the club so long after Trap left. At first, she thought he was just terribly drunk, and tried to let him sleep it off in a nearby hotel, but when he awoke, all hell broke loose.

When Bags opened his eyes after sleeping almost ten hours, and saw that he was surrounded by federal agents, he went hysterical. He started yelling for help, running into the bathroom and locking the door. He sat in the tub fully dressed with the hot water on until they convinced him they were not there to kill him. When he finally opened the door, soaking wet, they knew that something was wrong.

The doctors informed her once his blood test returned, that he had ingested numerous amounts of compound chemicals similar to those used to make the synthetic marijuana drug, K—2.

The whole misfortune of her rat going nuts put her back at point A. She knew Trap was responsible for his insanity, but she also knew she couldn't prove it. Standing next to her Grand Marquise, while deep in thought, she heard her phone ring.

"Agent Bradley here, what do you got for me?" She listened attentively as one of her fellow Agents informed her about the unsuccessful search of the strip club. No traces of K—2 was found on any of the cups throughout the establishment or in the trash. All the waitresses' statements seemed to corroborate each other's leaving her at a dead end.

"Damn it!" She shouted out of frustration, slamming her fist down on her roof.

"Can we at least bring the owner in?" she inquired, wanting to flex her federal muscle while she interrogated him for hours. After hearing it would do no good, she opened her car door and got in. After cranking the car up she cut her caller off in mid-sentence, "Don't worry about it. I'm going to find out who the fuck this Trap dude is and make him wish he never messed with the FBI."

***

Jasmin whined like a child desperately needing some attention. "Baby, come up stairs when y'all get through, because I gotta talk to you, okay?"

"Alright sweetheart," Cash replied as he watched her saunter back off towards the house.

Him and Trap was wrapping up what they had left to discuss, when she impolitely interrupted them. He forgot she had a present for him after returning from his trip to Miami.

So, after Trap replayed the events about what took place in the club, Cash filled him in on the meeting with Felix. He told him about how they kidnapped him from the hotel and how he assumed it was Manny. He wasn't ashamed to tell his friend that he was so scared his brain locked up.

He had already been through his fair share of traumatic experiences, so when this occurred, he thought his time clock was officially over.

Afterwards, he received the call from Trooper Stevens where he confirmed his long-arm reach of the law would extend to I-95. They were back in the game, and it was about time too because they were down to their last few bricks.

Trap's little hustlers were consuming the dope, and if it wasn't for the money they had for him every time he showed up, he would have thought they were eating the cocaine. His three partners from The Cross informed him the last time he stopped by, instead of coming once a week, he needed to come twice a week.

"Yeah, Big T," Outcast complained, "we been out of work for three days now, and I don't like tellin' our clientele we out, ya feel me?"

Trap smiled as he thought back to their conversation. He took pride serving them and considered the three of them his proteges. He knew when it came down to handling business, they would be on the clock, and not looking forward to clocking out.

"You heard me my nigga?" asked Cash, noticing the distant look in his eyes.

Trap nodded his head, not wanting to admit he didn't quite catch his last few words. "Yeah, yeah, my nigga," he replied unsure. "Felix gone take us to the top."

Cash just looked at him for a moment before laughing. He hadn't paid any attention to him as he tried telling him about Olivia. He knew right then it was time for him to go see what his baby wanted.

"Man, I'm gone cuzz," Cash dapped him up and walked back in the house to go see what Jasmin had for him. He wasn't about to keep her waiting any longer, and he could tell from Trap's posture and facial expression, he needed to go home and get some well needed rest.

When he stepped back in the crib, he noticed there was finally some peace and quiet around the place. He assumed Shay went back to Macon to spend time with her parents for the weekend, while his mom kept AJ. She kept him a lot, Cash believed, because of his resemblance to Money. It seemed like his mom was still trying to cope with the loss of her son, and everyone knew it.

When he got to the staircase, he noticed white and pink rose peddles sprinkled all the way to the top. That was a hint that Jasmin wanted to make love. It was her thing to make love on rose peddles because it made her feel like royalty. Ascending the staircase, he too began to feel like royalty, after thinking about the scene in Coming to America.

He heard Dru Hill's, 5 Steps, playing from their bedroom as he reached the top of the stairs. Attempting to tip toe into the room and sneak up on her, he slowly started peeling off his clothes. He kept his boxers on to give her a chance at taking something off. As he cracked the door, peaking into the room, he heard the jacuzzi running. He didn't see her in their round shaped king-sized bed, which she had the pleasure of decorating with a custom-made comforter from Pier One Imports. It was her signature to be laid across their bed wearing one of her laced Victoria Secret lingerie outfits, but not this time. As he headed over to the bathroom, she came from behind the door and snatched his boxer's down to his ankles. Out of reflex he reached down to pull them back up, but then he laughed after realizing she'd caught him slipping.

"I see you done started getting clever on me girl," he stated stepping out of the underwear and facing her.

She stood there wearing a pink one-piece lingerie set that was laced all over, exposing her breasts and crotch area. One of her legs was slightly bent in front of her as if she was attempting to pose for Dime Magazine. She wore her hair loosely but took some time to style it creatively on top of her head, leaving a few strands dangling on one side of her angelic face. Standing there taking in each other's presence, he admired her beauty.

As she stepped closer to him her heart rate sped up. This was the man she fought hard for, taking trips to see him while he was incarcerated, and fighting for his love. Cash was her man, and she loved him with all of her heart.

When they embraced, she kissed and licked all over his chiseled chest. With the steroids that the doctor prescribed him and the constant exercise routine he maintained in their home gym, Cash's body looked like the rapper, 50 Cent's after he got shot. Jasmin was pleased with his recovery. She took her time licking over his wound, caressing it with ease.

Grabbing ahold of her face he brought it next to his and they feverishly kissed. Their tongues danced around in each other's mouth as if they were exploring the new territory. After five minutes of their lip locking, she pushed him onto their bed, his dick now standing at twelve o'clock. Grabbing it, she placed it into her warm mouth. Although she knew it would have felt better inside her warm kitten, she wanted to please her king. Feeling his body tense-up, then relax, she took her time and eased him down her throat. His eyes closed as her head bobbed up and down to the beat of the music.

She wouldn't have time tonight to tell him about their baby on the way, because she planned on making love to him all night long. So, her plan was to put him to sleep, then tell him in the morning.

CHAPTER 9

NETWORK

"Patricia Lanett Brown!" the Dean announced, while the crowd cheered loudly. Peaches strutted across the stage, head held high, as she was presented with her bachelor's degree in Criminal Justice.

"Wooooooo, you go girl!" Shay and Mercedees screamed and yelled from the stands when she received her four-year degree.

People from all over packed the Oliver Auditorium. Some had come from as far as Spokane, Washington, to support their loved one while they were being honored at their graduation. Shay and Mercedees were right there, side by side, with Peaches's family as they continued shouting from their section. Everyone was so proud of her, and they couldn't wait to tell her how cute she looked in her cap and gown. She had finally graduated from Spelmen.

"Wooooo!" They continued shouting after another person received their degree.

It was a major day for all recipients, so they showed their support for the other girls as well. It was the unity and girl power they encouraged at the school. Black women were the mavericks in today's corporate America, and they wanted it to be known.

When they called the last recipient up to receive their degree, everyone gave them a loud round of applause. They could see that Peaches was down at the bottom hugging all of her classmates as they celebrated. After everyone settled down, they started directing them towards the hallway for refreshments, giving the graduates a chance to spend time with their family.

***

"Wooooo, diva!" Mercedees and Shay ran up to Peaches and hugged her, screaming as if they'd won the lottery. "Girl, we are so proud of you."

"Girl," she boasted cheerfully, "I can't believe it!"

They took turns taking pictures with her, while she held up her degree.

"Where's everybody?" She asked, looking around the crowded hallway for her family.

"Girl, we hauled ass and left them once we seen them releasing y'all," Shay informed her, "but come on, I'm sure they're around here somewhere."

Making their way through the congested crowd, Peaches felt somebody tug on her shirt. When she turned around to see who it was, her eyes nearly popped out of her head.

"Congratulations!" Jasmin cheered hesitantly, as Peaches eyed her suspiciously.

When Shay and Mercedees turned around, they noticed Peaches was no longer behind them. So, they pried their way back over to where she was. Making their way through the crowd, both gasped at the sight of Jasmine. They told her their plans were to attend Peaches's graduation, but never expected for her to show up. It was an awkward moment for everyone. They just hoped Peaches's had enough since not to start a round two at her graduation.

As Peaches eyes narrowed at her archnemesis, she began to feel her blood boil. This was the THOT that stole her man's heart, and she wasn't over it yet. Before she got a chance to cuss her out, Jasmin spoke first.

"I come in peace, Peaches," she said humbly, raising her hand to give Peaches a graduation gift.

Peaches stood there frozen. Was this really happening? or, was this some kind of sick joke? For a second, she expected Ashton Kutcher to pop up with his crew of camera men, and inform her that she'd just been *Punked*, but that was not going to happen.

As she pondered the idea of punching Jasmin in the face, she spoke again.

"I'm sorry," she sincerely apologized, still holding the gift out for her to receive.

That made Peaches's whole demeanor change. She couldn't believe what had just come out of Jasmin's mouth. It was the most shocking thing to happen to her all year. For years she hated this girl and although she felt like that, she knew deep down in her heart, it wasn't her fault that she lost the only man she truly loved.

Shay and Mercedees were staring at the two of them, slowly moving into position just in case Peaches decided to turn her graduation into a UFC match. Shay was going to grab Peaches, while Mercedees grabbed Jasmine, however, something extraordinary took place after what seemed like hours of silence between the rivals. Peaches grabbed the gift from her hand and opened it. Inside of the Kay Jeweler's gift box was a princess cut diamond neckless with a half heart shaped blue charm attached to it. It was trimmed in white gold and twinkled at her from every angle.

Shay and Mercedees, stood beside Peaches so they could view the pricy gift. After reading the inscription on the back of the neckless, she looked back up at her. Jasmin was smiling because she knew Peaches would understand what the inscription meant.

"Shared love," she whispered to herself. She knew exactly what it meant. It was Jasmin's way of telling her that he still had feelings for her. She didn't know what to say. Not in a million years would she have expected her to do something like this, and because she did, Peaches decided to bury the hate she had towards her. She reached out and hugged Jasmine. When they embraced, they both shared tears of joy for finally forgiving one another.

"Ahhhhhh," Mercedees and Shay sighed as they went over and joined them in a group hug.

***

Trap rocked his head from side-to-side as he listened to J. Coles "No life better than yours". He was on his way to see Jay, one of Cash's homeboys from prison, and he needed to keep his mind at peace. Everything, so far, was going good. They were expecting a call from Felix any day now regarding the shipment of cocaine, and where to pick it up. Cash had given him contact info to another one of his homies from West Palm Beach to call and organize a hub. After linking up with him, Trap, wasn't so sure, Smoke was the right person for the job.

He had drove down there 2 days ago and talked to the dark-skinned dread headed thug, and his first impression of Smoke wasn't a good one. Knocking on the door of the duplex apartment he told him to meet him at, Trap noticed the poor condition it was in. The exterior was dusty and beat up and the apartment appeared abandoned. There were holes in the screen door and the paint on the walls looked old. It was really something, and if this was where the dude Smoke lived, Trap was going to have a hard time trusting Cash's judgment.

When somebody finally opened the door, he saw what appeared to be a black African holding an AK—47 assault rifle. That sent major alarms off in his head because he had called Smoke an hour prior to showing up so it wouldn't be any problems. A little reluctant, he asked for Smoke. The guy at the door told him to hold on, then closed the door back. Trap thought about leaving at that very moment, but before he could make up his mind, stepping off the porch to leave, Smoke came from around the side of the apartment.

"Yo, what up! " He greeted Trap, stepping over some shrubs before giving him some dap.

"You, Smoke?" Trap asked, questionably overlooking the guy.

"Is you, Trap?", he replied, answering a question with a question.

Trap wasn't feeling his vibe, but he proceeded to talk with him. He informed Smoke about Cash's intention of putting him in a position to win, but due to his sudden death, he never got a chance to. He broke down how everything was still in motion, but instead of Cash being there to execute it, he was there as his trustee. Smoke kept asking questions about what happened to Cash, but Trap could only give him so much information. After a while, he got tired of going back and forth with him and said, "So, what's up? Are you in, or are you out?"

Smoke was insulted by his need for an answer. He knew Cash could be the only one to tell him about their time in Victorville, and since Cash was his man, he stated, "Fo show, my nigga, straight like dat!"

They both nodded in agreement, dapping each other. He asked Smoke how he planned on storing everything after receiving the work, and after hearing his plan, Trap felt confident about the situation. So, after the details were discussed, he left West Palm feeling a little better about doing business with Smoke and scheduled to meet up with Cash's other homie in Fayetteville, NC.

After exiting I-95 and picking up his phone, scrolling down his contact list, Trap pressed the call button for Jay.

"Aye, where you at?" Jay answered the phone.

"I'll be there in about 40 minutes," he replied.

"Alright then, I'll be standing outside when you pull up." 'Thank God?' Trap thought to himself, "Alright, bruh." When he arrived, Jay was standing outside a decent looking two story home talking to a young chick. Trap parked his Mazerati next to the curb and got out. Trap smirked as he noticed Jay and the girl eyeing him a little too hard.

Approaching Jay, he watched as he attempted to usher the light-skinned chick away, but she wasn't trying to go anywhere.

"Damn dawg," Jay said, walking up to greet him. "I didn't know you were gonna pull up like this." He leaned to the side so he could get a better look at the lavish ride.

"Oh, this shit," he replied nonchalantly, glancing over his shoulder, "Man, this my everyday right here."

"Well, it sure is nice," the light skinned girl chimed in, smiling as she watched Trap.

Jay turned around with a mug on his face and shouted, "Shanda, you better get the fuck out of here!"

She stormed off, clearly upset he embarrassed her like that. She was his little cousin, not his daughter, and she planned on telling him about himself later. As she marched through the yard and down the street, Trap took notice of her fat ass.

"That's your girl, huh?"

"Nah, that's my lil cousin," he stated, "she just nosy as hell. I'll be glad when she go off to college so I ain't gotta worry about one of these clowns around here sticking their dick in her."

Trap nodded his head, pleased by his concern for his family.

"But fuck all that," he continued, dismissing the situation as if it was nothing. "Let's sit on the porch and talk about what you got on deck." He walked towards the porch and gestured for Trap to follow him.

On his way up the sidewalk, Trap checked out the surroundings. The neighborhood seemed quiet, and he remembered seeing a few old folks outside watering their lawn as he drove down the street. Everything gave off a tranquil setting, but Trap knew better. If a person wanted to catch you slipping, this would definitely be the way to rock them to sleep. So, before he sat down in the plastic chair, he touched the side of his waist to make sure his Glock 22 was secure in its holster.

For the first 30 minutes, he ran down Cash's plan. He told Jay how Cash always talked about him and a few other people he was incarcerated with. When he got to the part about the melee between them and the D.C. boys, they shared a good laugh. He could tell by Jay's demeanor and humbleness, he was a quiet dude, and Trap liked quietness. When he described the assassination, Jay expressed his condolences. He liked Cash a lot, and to hear of his fatal demise was heartbreaking.

"Man, that was a good nigga," he commented sadly.

They shared a moment of silence as they thought back on some of the memories and experiences they had with Cash. Trap didn't know if it was him, or was his skills just that nice, because every time he had to convince someone Cash was dead, he got better at it.

They continued their conversation for another 2 hours as Trap explained in detail how much money he was looking to make if he decided to get down with the program. It was a deal of a lifetime, and all it required was for him to set up shop, and issue out bricks to customers in the Carolinas, Virginia, and Tennessee. It was every dope boy dream to eventually start moving units, and now that he had his chance, he was going to take it.

"How long will it take for me to snatch one of them?" He asked, pointing over towards the Mazerati.

Trap smiled.

"A few days my nigga, just a few days."

***

"Bring his ass over here!" Agent Bradley ordered the U.S. Marshall.

They had just completed their third bust of the day, and she was not tired. She had been on a rampage for weeks, cracking down on every dope house around Chatham County. Her impetus for catching drug dealers had intensified after Trap slipped through her fingers. Although all the other agents in her office touted her for coming so close to catching him, she wasn't satisfied. Her conscious was eating at her soul. Every time she closed her eyes to get some sleep, she would see her big brother. It was like he was tormenting her from the grave. She stayed in a state of depression because she believed she was disappointing him. To keep her focused on the job, continuing the pursuit for her brother's killer, she took Risperdal and dranked plenty of coffee. It was the only thing that would give her a piece of mind.

When the marshal walked her latest victim over to her car, she grabbed the drug dealer by the collar of his Akoo shirt and growled, "Do you know where Trap is?" She had the look of a blood thirsty animal, so the dealer thought real long and hard before he replied.

"Never heard of him."

She fumed from frustration, shoving him back over into the deputy's custody. She didn't have time for their games. Somebody knew where Trap was and if someone didn't speak up soon, she was going to lose it.

When she returned to her vehicle, she pounded on the steering wheel while yelling and screaming to herself. Some of the law enforcement personnel, along with some of the perpetrators from the raid, stared at her. Nobody wanted any dealings with the federal officer who was clearly out of her mind.

CHAPTER 10

LOVE

It was pitch black outside, and they had been waiting for hours. Felix contacted Cash less than 48 hours later about where to pick up the shipment, and here they were in Florida, sitting by a pier in a Box-truck truck. Trap and Smoke were both looking across the Gulf of Mexico for any kind of signal. They zoomed in and out with their high-powered binoculars as they watched the massive body of water wander aimlessly along the southeastern seaboard. They knew at any minute it would be there, so they remained calm, and continued watching.

"Right there," said Trap, pointing into the darkness, "you see that?"

For a minute, Smoke couldn't see anything. He didn't know if Trap that was tripping, or whether he was just blind. Then, all of a sudden, he saw it.

"Yeah, I see it," he spoke in a low tone, placing the binoculars under his seat. There was someone in the water flickering a reflector back and forth trying to get their attention. He got out of the truck and walked down to the end of the dock. When he saw the reflection again with his natural eye, he took his cell phone out and waved it back and forth above his head. When they stopped signaling, he did the same. He knew any minute now, they would have over a ton of cocaine in their possession, and although he couldn't wait, he did begin to get a little nervous.

In the truck, Trap saw Smoke signal for him to come down with the pallet jack they had on the back of the truck, but before he got out and grabbed it, he got on his walkie talkie, and instructed everyone to move into position.

Up in the front, at both entrances to the pier, he had armed men in two black SUV's watching the road. They were security just in case anything went wrong. They were loaded down with level two bullet proof vests and fully automatic machine guns equipped with silencers. Trap gave them specific instructions to gun down anybody who looked suspicious. At 2:45 in the morning, they didn't expect for anyone to be walking around down by the water, but if by chance someone did to wander too close, their security detail was ready to eliminate the threat.

A little further on up the road, sitting in a Florida State Trooper's vehicle, was their private escort. The State Trooper, Trooper Stevens arranged to escort them was instructed to tail the Box-truck up I-95 until it crossed into Georgia. His job entailed listening to his scanner and alerting the driver of the Box-truck if any trouble was up ahead. If there was, they would get off on the very next exit, and wait until he informed them the coast was clear. He was to be compensated twenty—five thousand for his day's work. Once they made their first drop off in West Palm Beach, it would be a straight shot from there to Savannah. The trooper agreed to escort them as far as Duval County, then his job would be done.

Trap already had another trooper lined up to escort him to Savannah once he reached the Georgia state line. Their plan was going to go smoothly, and he had no doubts about their capability of being able to move that much work. By statistics, the United States consumed on average around fifty—thousand pounds of cocaine a month, and with those numbers he knew there was no way in hell they would have a hard time getting rid of the bricks. It was all about supply and demand, and they looked forward to being the suppliers that met those demands.

Trap maneuvered the lift all the way down the pier until he stood next to Smoke. They eyed the water for another 15 minutes before they saw it.

When the top of a mini submarine raised up out of the water, they both smiled.

Watching the hatch popped open then a dark-skinned Mexican's head appeared out of it as it continued floating closer and closer towards them.

From the surface, it seemed as if he was coming out a drainage pipe that was connected somewhere under the dock. When it reached them, they bent down and lifted him up out of the sub.

"Gracias amigos," he thanked them, "tus hablan espanol?" They stared at him for a second, then looked at each other. They didn't think they needed to know Spanish. That was something Trap never anticipated; however, he knew exactly what to do. While the Mexican stood there with a stupid looking grin on his face, he pulled out his phone and called Cash. After explaining the situation to him he handed the Mexican the phone. Smoke was busy helping his other two compadres climb out of the sub.

"Damn y'all stink!" Smoke complained, pulling his shirt collar over his nose, attempting to muffle the repugnant odor.

As he hoisted the third passenger up, he said, "Aye migo, you need a bath."

The happy-go-lucky Mexican smiled in return, completely oblivious to what smoke was suggesting. He was just glad to be in the U.S.

The first Mexican walked back over to Trap and handed him the phone after speaking to Cash. He said something in Spanish before pointing to the sub and saying one-thousand kilos. Trap knew right then, Cash had confirmed what they were waiting on.

The Mexican went back over towards the sub and began barking orders to his compadres. They hurriedly jumped back into the sub, and 5 by 5, started passing the kilos out the top of the sub. They made an assembly line, working vigorously together as they passed the keys down to Trap as he neatly stacked them onto a pallet. When he finished the first one, he ran back over to the truck and grabbed a long box of ceram wrap. Him and Smoke carefully wrapped the plastic around the loaded pallet until the whole thing felt sturdy enough to move. After loading it onto the truck, he grabbed another pallet and took it down the pier, continuing the same process three more times. It took them a little over an hour to complete the task.

When everything was finished and all the dope was loaded onto the truck, Trap handed each one of the Mexicans twenty-five hundred and took off. It was understood they were to receive twenty-five when they left Mexico, and twenty-five when they arrived in the States.

When Trap and Smoke got back into the truck, he got on the walkie talkie and said, "Alpha, bravo, charlie, are we clear?" One-by-one, they radioed back that the coast was clear.

For the next two hours, they discussed the details of their agreement. After arriving in West Palm, Smoke took one pallet, totaling two—hundred and fifty kilograms, and broke it down. He was instructed to test the quality of each brick before removing 6 ounces and replacing it with 6 ounces of quinine. Then he was to compress it back to its original form. Since the dope was so pure, Cash knew they could take out a few ounces and nobody would even notice, turning one-thousand kilos into eleven-hundred and seventy. Once he was finished, he was to take the labels Trap gave him, and stamp each brick. Each kilo would be stamped according to its area of distribution, with oranges representing Florida, peaches representing Georgia, and so forth. It was to ensure that each hub had its own label. That way, if any cocaine was returned to their organization, they could deal with that specific hub accordingly.

When they made it to Smoke's duplex, Trap backed the truck into the area on the side of the apartment. After the pallet was unloaded, they rolled the Box-truck's door down and parted ways, but not before handing Smoke a new phone.

"Call me from this phone when you're done," he told him before hopping back into the truck and taking off. There were three more drop offs to make before the day was over and he needed to get them done as soon as possible.

***

Exiting his truck, Trap walked into Tameka's house and took a seat on her couch. It had been a long day and he needed to unwind.

"I'm in the kitchen, Travis," she shouted after hearing him enter her home.

That was his cue to close his eyes and get some rest.

Trap was on his way to Cash's house when Tameka called and asked him to come over. She had picked up the newest Kings of Comedy DVD and wanted him to come by and enjoy it with her, so after he made the last drop-off in New York he headed over to her house. His trip along I-95 was escorted the whole way but cost damn near three-hundred thousand. Each State Trooper had his own particular price tag for their protection, however, Trap knew every penny was worth it.

As he sat there enjoying the sweet aroma of Tameka's cooking, he began dozing off.

"Ugh!" He grunted from the weight of his little cousin Quay jumping on. "Boy is you crazy?" Trap laughed, picking him up and tickling him. He was wide awake now at the sight of his little soldier.

"Ha ha ha!" Quay giggled childishly as Trap continued tickling his sides, making him laugh uncontrollably. "Big T, Okaaaaaay," he pleaded for Trap to stop.

"Why you surprise me like that?" he asked, smiling.

Quay shrugged his shoulders and giggled as if he had no clue why he did it.

Trap knew he was happy to see him. Ever since his daddy got locked up, he's been a father figure to Quay. On every birth- day and Christmas, he would come through the door bearing gifts for Quay and his mother. They were his closest relatives, and he made sure they never needed for anything.

"Where's your virtual reality game I bought you last month?" Trap asked.

Quay pointed towards the back of the house, so they headed off to his room in search of it. After locating the gaming device, they played with his Oculus headset for about 30 minutes before Tameka shouted from the kitchen for them to come eat. Quay led the way down the trailer's hallway where his mom had his food already sitting at his personal Spiderman table.

"Thanks, Meeka," Trap said, grabbing his plate and returning to the living room.

"What do you want to drink?" She asked, sticking her head around the partition.

"Just bring me some water," he replied between bites.

The beef ribs and baked macaroni and cheese she cooked was off the chain. He was devouring the meal as if he was participating in an eating contest. By the time she brought his glass of water he had one third of his plate left.

"Dang boy," she laughed, staring at him, "you must ain't ate nothin' all day?"

He stopped eating and asked sarcastically, "You can tell?"

They chuckled at his quip remark.

Once they were all through eating, Quay joined them on the couch. She grabbed the remote form the table and directed the DVR to play the movie. For the next three hours, they laughed nonstop, enjoying the jokes of Mike Epps, D-Ray, and Katt Williams. By the time it was over, Quay had fallen asleep between them. So, Meeka picked him up and put him to bed.

When she returned, she saw that Trap had fallen asleep too with his head leaned back on the couch. She smiled at peaceful he looked, walking off to grab a blanket from out of the hallway closet. She covered him up and kissed him on the cheek like she did her son a few moments earlier, but instead of walking off she watched him rest. She had an emotional attachment to him that she didn't quite understand. Trap had all the qualities of a real man, and she loved that about him. So, instead of suppressing her emotions any longer, she decided to act on them.

She gently began kissing him, hoping he would wake up and kiss her back. Seeing how he wouldn't budge, she removed the blanket and sat down straddling him. Placing her arms around his head, she leaned forward to where their faces were just inches apart. For a minute she just looked at him. Trap was her 2nd generation cousin, and she knew what she was doing was wrong, but her heart told her she needed him. He was everything she wanted in a man. He cared for her and her son like no other man had ever done before. Sure, Quan did pay the bills and all that, but what she never told Trap was that he was abusive towards her. She knew if he were to ever find out, he would make sure her baby daddy saw a graveyard instead of a prison cell. Then on top of that, her father was even worst.

Growing up, her father would always slide in her room while her mother was at work and sexually molest her. For a while, she didn't think anything was wrong with it, interpreting it as her daddy showing her love. But one day, she watched a girl, not too much older than her at the time, go on Dr. Phil and re—tell her story. It brought tears to her eyes when she heard how her, and the girl shared similar stories. From that moment on, she screamed at the top of her lungs when she saw him. When her mother came home, she tried telling her how he sexually molested her all those years, but she didn't believe here.

After that, he never touched her again, but her relationship with her mother would never be the same. They argued and fought all the time, until one day she decided at the age of fifteen, to move out. She stayed at some friends and relatives houses until she met Quan. Then, that's when she got pregnant. Never hesitating to move with him out to Dublin, she packed her bags, and got the hell on.

So, now that she was in a position to finally give someone she could trust, her heart, she acted on her emotions. As she leaned a little closer into him, sliding her tongue around his thick lips, he stirred a little before she went all the way in, completely sticking her tongue in his mouth. Trap instantly awoke, but didn't open his eyes, enjoying the warmth of a woman's embrace. His hands caressed her body while their tongues danced around in each other's mouth. When he finally decided to open his eyes, it hit him like a Mac truck doing a 100 miles per hour.

"Tameka?" He murmured questionably, trying to hold her back, "What are you doing cuzz?" He couldn't believe she was just throwing herself on him like that.

"Baby don't stop," she begged, gazing into his eyes as he held her back from kissing him.

He attempted to get up, but she threw her weight forward onto him, making him sit back down. She grabbed ahold of his face and looked into his eyes. His dick was rock hard, and he didn't know if he could control himself any longer.

"Listen," she pleaded for him to calm down, "Travis, I am in love with you, don't you see that?"

He couldn't believe it. Looking into her eyes he knew she was telling the truth. She really was in-love with him, and when he opened his mouth to tell her that what they were doing was wrong, she leaned forward and passionately kissed him. At that point he couldn't control his emotions any longer. She was awakening a hormonal beast inside him that was driving him wild. Deep down, he faulted himself for being so vulnerable. It had been six months since he had sex and didn't realize how much he was missing the human-to-human interaction.

Unable to fight the internal desire any longer, he kissed her back, pulling off her pink tank top so he could suck on her nickel sized nipples. Glad that she was able to get him to submit, she greedily reached down between them and unbuckled his pants, unleashing his manhood. She quickly placed it inside her warm wet pussy, pushing the polyester boy shorts she was wearing to the side.

They groaned from the sensation of being a perfect fit. As they continued feverishly kissing, she slowly rocked back and forth on his dick. They both knew there was no turning back. They had crossed a bridge in their relationship that would never allow them to remain cousins. There was no need for them to act like family anymore, because from this day forward they be considered lovers.

***

"Are you serious? Your dad's a US Senator," he stated unbelievably.

"As serious as an ISIS terrorist strapped with a bomb," Olivia replied metaphorically. "Matter of fact," she continued, "he's one of the first Hispanics to hold office now for almost two decades."

Cash shook his head, "That's crazy!"

She had called him earlier while he was out riding his four-wheeler, but due to the loud motor, he missed her call. When he finally stopped and noticed he had missed calls from Trap and Olivia, he called her back first because if Trap urgently needed to speak with him, he would have called him more than once.

"Mhmmmm hmmmm," she muttered, waiting on him to end the brief silence between them.

"Well," he began, realizing she was waiting on him, "I remember you telling me about a few franchises you owned. How are they coming along? I'm pretty sure they keep you busy."

She enjoyed the sound of his voice, "Yeah they do, but I'd prefer it if it was you that kept me busy."

He was flattered, but he knew how much of a good woman he had at home.

"Yeah," he replied, not knowing what to say next, "but you know I'm."

"Already taken," she interjected. "Oh my God! What happened to the days when people just had fun sometimes? It's not like your married yet or anything like that. I just want to enjoy myself with a man I know would appreciate me. Am I wrong for that?"

'Hell nawl!' he thought to himself. Although Cash would have loved to tap that ass, he couldn't. He had to be responsible for at the end of the day. He liked the amiable relationship they were developing, because it was completely harmless, but he couldn't think with his little head and he knew it.

Glancing around the forestry that surrounded him as if he was watching out for Jasmin, he said, "So, what kind of franchises did you say they were?"

She chuckled at his attempt to steer the conversation away from what she wanted to talk about.

"Clever," she complimented him, "I own a few organic cosmetic shops along the east coast."

"Really," he replied, sounding impressed.

"Yeah, we specialize in making different kinds of soaps, toothpastes, shampoos, and whatever else someone may need to improve their hygiene. Everything in my shops are natural and organic. No animal fat or anything of that nature either."

"So, who develops all the ingredients to make it all work?"

"We do," she replied abruptly, "I have my own chemists who operate out of my test lab in New York, Virginia, and Florida. That's one of the reasons I was in Florida when you met me. I was down there checking on a new product we planned on advertising soon."

"Yeah, what will that be?"

"Baby products," she answered cheerfully.

He was thinking while she was talking. She had caught his interest when she talked about her laboratories along the East Coast. Hell, he had cocaine distribution locations around those same areas. He secretly wondered if she could be of any use to him and his organization. By her father being a US Congressman, surely no one would suspect her of engaging in the trafficking of narcotics. So, it was an idea that definitely crossed his mind, but he wasn't convinced that she would be willing to participate.

For another hour he sat on his four-wheeler and tried feeling her out. She seemed like a spoiled little rich girl who was down for getting a little dirty, but he had to make sure first she had the potential to be a real criminal. In any drug trafficking enterprise, it took for everyone to know what was at stake for everything run smoothly. No mistakes, not failures, and especially no snitching. This is what took down all the great drug lords and kingpins in the U.S.

Cash would not be so quick to leap out there on a whim after learning from those historical figures what mistakes not to make. He knew better, and by knowing better, he planned on doing better. Olivia did have his mind at work though, and if she could convince him that she was down like four flat tires, then he would put her to work.

CHAPTER 11

BABY GIRL

Mercedees was enjoying her summer break. Her first year at Spelman came with many challenges and plenty of obstacles, but she was able to pull through. After watching Peaches walk across that stage to receive her degree, her mind was made up. She was fully determined to getting her own degree, and she'd be damned if she let anyone get in her way. She busted her ass and caught up with schoolwork. The time she spent away was detrimental to her GPA, and she needed to fix that. So, until it was time for final exams, she worked on homework assignments, essays, and quizzes to bring her GPA back to where she had it. She didn't have time for anyone or anything else. The makeup work she had to was complete was intense, but it was necessary. This was why she tried so hard during her pre—college years to learn as much as possible. Her high expectations of excelling in class and graduating Magna Cum Laude motivated her to stay centered. She was determined not to let that vision be distorted or altered by anyone, and she meant that.

For a while, she rode around the busy streets of Atlanta, taking in the diverse scene. The big city had a lot to offer anyone trying to come up. People from all over, including India, Sudan, and Asia, were migrating to the Black Mecca in order to make a living for themselves. It was the norm around the South for anyone to walk into a convenience store and hear one of the employees ask, "Can I help you my friend?" People from all nationalities and different cultures made their way from their in``digenous lands to capitalize off of the United States resources. The atmosphere was harmonic, and everybody got along. Atlanta was definitely the place to be if you were trying to do something with yourself, that's why Mercedees kept her head held high as she cruised the streets in her drop top Lexus. She was the shit, and she knew it. While all the other girls at her school struggled to pay their tuition, she struggled to find the right outfit to buy. She was not hurting for money thanks to her brothers, but she was no stranger to living under the poverty level either. Not too long ago, she could remember how her mother turned a simple Ramen noodle soup into a shrimp pasta meal. She laughed to herself as she thought back to those times. The project days is what she called them.

Now, times where different. She was someone of another status, and she enjoyed her affluent lifestyle. It was what her brothers worked hard for, and sadly given their life for.

As she passed the drive-in movie theater, she thought she saw Darryl's car pulling in, so she made a u—turn to find out. She wasn't sure if it was his car or not, but she to know. There was, from what she could see, two people in the car and she wanted to make sure he wasn't playing any games.

He told her that she was the only person he was messing around with, and she wanted to believe him, but her intuition was kicking the door in to her emotions. Their relationship had gotten a little deeper since she moved back to the A, and since he was doing everything he could to please her, she wanted to make sure he was doing right by her. She appreciated a man who knew how to take care of a lady and Darryl was turning out to be something special, however, she didn't tolerate cheating.

So, until she was confident he was keeping it real, she was going to investigate and find out the truth. When she made it to the entrance, she paid the cashier the going rate for a movie, and pulled in. She had no clue as to what section he could've went to, or even if it was really him for that matter, but she was going to ride around until she located that car. She stopped at one of the concession stands to grab a bag of popcorn just in case it turned out not be him. That way, she could sit back and enjoy her movie instead.

After driving around for fifteen minutes, she couldn't locate the car and thought maybe her eyes was playing tricks on her, until she saw it ducked off in the corner. She didn't want to make a scene, pulling up in front of it and getting out, so she found a parking spot somewhere nearby. It was getting darker by the minute as the sun began to fade off into the west, so she got out after parking her convertible and slowly made her way down the row of cars. If it turned out not to be his car, she was just going to keep on walking by like she was lost and return to her vehicle. But if she discovered him with some THOT, she was going to make him pay.

Walking by it the first time didn't go so well. She noticed there was a guy sitting on the passenger side with his head laid back like he was asleep, but from what she could see, nobody was sitting on the driver side. However, when she looked at the rims, she knew for sure that it was his car. That persuaded her to turn around and follow her intuition. As she walked back up and approached the car, she bent down and squinted her eyes to get a better peek. She watched in shock as the passenger guided someone's head up and down into his lap obviously sucking his dick. At that moment, she didn't know what to think standing there in front of the car identical to her man's. The passenger had no clue she was standing there either, because he was in total bliss enjoying his fallacio. The curiosity was beginning to kill her. She needed to know if her mind was playing tricks on her, so she walked around to the driver's side door, her heart beating faster and faster with every step.

"Darryl!" She shouted in disbelief.

Darryl quickly lifted his head up out of the man's lap at the sound of his name and looked around. He couldn't believe he'd been caught. When he saw the expression on Jasmin's face, all the blood drained from his.

"Oh my god!" she panicked, not wanting to believe her eyes. "Oh my god, Darryl!"

"Baby," he called after her, opening his door to get out, "it's not what it looks like," he tried to explain, getting out and cautiously approaching her.

"Don't you fuckin' touch me!" she warned, shaking from the state of shock as she backed away from him.

He stopped approaching her, but continued to explain. "Listen, Mercedees, I didn't mean for this to happen." They were beginning to attract an audience now as people started getting out of their cars to watch the latest Maury episode. Mercedees was still trying to process fact that Darryl was gay. To know that a guy she was having sex with, liked dick as much as she did was crazy. The scene of his head bouncing up and down, replayed over and over again in her mind. She felt queasy and her world was spinning out of control, and before she knew it, her breakfast and lunch came spewing out her mouth. Darryl had made her sick. The sight of him gave her an upset stomach and she couldn't stand the sight of him any longer.

***

"Man, what the fuck is she doing?" TP asked his homeboys as they sat in the car watching Mercedees throw up.

"Nawl, man," Square replied blowed, just now realizing what she was doing. He nodded his head in sheer disbelief, "she's throwing up dawg."

All three of them were watching through their binoculars and they didn't know what was going on until they saw Darryl get out his car. All they knew was that Mercedees was walking around the parking lot looking suspect. They knew she was looking for someone by the way she was creeping around, but they didn't know who.

"No fuckin way," Juvi added, looking at his other two homeboys, "this nigga's a fag!" he concluded after watching the passenger of Darryl's car get out and straighten his pants.

They all bust out laughing. It was too much for them to watch. They had heard about Atlanta's LGBTQ community, but to witness it like this was unbelievable.

They were still laughing about it when they heard her scream. As they looked back over to where she was through their binoculars, they saw her swinging left and right at Darryl. He was trying his best to dodge her, but she kept coming. As her punches were connecting, hitting him upside the head, the passenger ran over and grabbed her from behind.

Without anything else being said, they jumped out of the truck, and ran over there.

***

Everything was going great. Their distribution network was moving smoothly and everyone was making money. Felix called Cash on a regular basis, commending him on his brilliance. Thanks to him, he was shipping more cocaine into the US than all of his other competitors. Shipments weren't being lost, and the demand for the product was increasing. They upgraded from moving a ton a month, to 3 tons a month. It seemed like overnight, Jay and Smoke had become millionaires, along with Twan and JJ.

Trap couldn't afford to keep taking trips back and forth to New York delivering dope when he had to focus on the hub in Savannah. So, he got Twan and JJ to move up north, while him and Outkast took care of the business around the Seaport. Usually, he wouldn't have trusted two workers that were just now becoming a part of their organization with such responsibility, however, their resume from Tha Cross spoke volumes to him and he felt like they were the best ones for the job. The thought had crossed his mind about using Damage and Tru at first, but after giving it some in-depth thought, he knew it would be best to keep them in Georgia. He needed them close to him just in case things got out of hand. They had proven themselves to be reliable and trustworthy, but Trap knew they were better off being nearby for strategic purposes.

For the next 6 months, everything went according to plan. Smoke picked up the shipment from the docks, taking it back with him to West Palm Beach. From there, Trap would have Damage and Tru escort the rest of it up along the coast. They dropped a quarter of the load off at every hub until they were completely out. There was so much coke out on the streets, the price of a kilo had decreased dramatically from thirty thousand, to twenty—two thousand. Everyone was glad the streets were flooded again. More and more money was coming in. From the kingpins to the smokers, everybody was happy. Trap even hired a crew to count all the small bills because the work was so over-bearing. Their organization was beginning to reach new heights in the underground drug trade, and they didn't even notice it. Cash and Trap were so dedicated towards getting revenge, they hadn't even noticed the massive size of wealth they'd begun to accumulate. To avoid getting on the Fed's radar, they kept their money stored in offshore accounts in Panama, Switzerland, and the Cayman Islands.

Every single one of their family members had a trust-fund set up in their name within those countries. They were a force to be reckoned with, and they couldn't wait to exert some of that force on Migo and his uncles. But until then, they had dope to move.

"Yeah, I think we just might be able to use her, bruh," Cash told Trap as they sat in his living room discussing business.

"Man, listen, I'm more so wandering towards the old saying homie, 'why fix it when it ain't broke?'" He was clearly skeptical about the idea Cash was proposing.

Cash nodded his head, acknowledging his concern.

"But shit," he replied, "aren't you getting tired of taking the chance of a shipment getting knocked off? I mean, everything seems fine right now my nigga, but old moves leave room for new mistakes, ya feel me?"

Cash knew their whole network was fine, but it was also beginning to get played out. He wanted to make their trafficking as easy as possible, and after speaking with Olivia about bringing her in as a partner, he thought it would be a wise decision switch up their method. The quarter million they were dishing out to the State Patrol's Office had increased, and he didn't see it going any lower anytime soon. Once they heard about how the streets were inundated with cocaine, they decided to increase their security fee, bringing their 6-figure contract to a 7-figure one.

Cash and Trap wasn't really tripping, because they knew how important the troopers were to their operation. They needed them more than anything, but if this deal went through with Olivia, Cash would have to send them all away with a nice severance package.

"Man, I don't know about that my nigga," Trap replied indecisively, not liking the idea of them bringing her into their organization.

"Why do you want this bitch in our game room anyway?"

They both turned around when they heard the door swing open.

In came Jasmin and Shay, followed by Ms. Tina, who was holding AJ. They were coming back from the family reunion gathering they were having up the street. Each one of them were holding some plates of food as they walked right in the kitchen, not paying Cash or Trap any mind.

"I hope y'all brought us something to eat?" Cash asked, looking over at Trap, smiling.

"Baby, you know I got y'all something," Jasmin assured him, walking over to where he was seated and pecked him on the lips.

"How's my baby girl doing?" he asked, pulling her towards him and placing his head next to her protruding belly.

She was expecting to have the baby in a few more weeks, and he couldn't wait. He was a little disappointed when the doctor informed them they were having a little girl, but he kept it to himself. Whether it's girl or boy, he would love the child all the same. He planned on trying again in the near future, because a junior to carry on his legacy was what he was looking for.

"Boy please," she said, rubbing his head as he waited for the baby inside her to move, "this lil heffa probably sleep after all the food I done fed her lil greedy ass."

"Well, as long as my baby don't come out obese, she can eat whateva she wants."

Trap cleared his throat to get Cash's attention.

"Oh, my bad dawg," Cash apologized, standing up to kiss Jasmin once more time. "Baby, we gone be in the game room if you need me, okay." He walked around her and gestured for Trap to follow him so they could finish their conversation. What they had to discuss was important, so he ended the moment he was sharing with Jasmin and their baby and headed off towards the basement.

When they made it to the stairwell, Cash clicked the light and opened the door. They walked down the wooden steps until they reached the concrete floor, then Cash led the way through the basement to another door where he pulled out his keys and opened it so they could go in inside. The room contained a pool table and two 72-inch HD TV's that were mounted on opposite walls. A PlayStation 5 was connected to one of them, while an Xbox Millennium was connected to the other. There was also a mini bar in the corner with two bar stools in front of it, two bean bag chairs and two recliners positioned in front of the TV's. It was a comfortable environment to conduct business.

They both walked over towards the bar and took a seat. Trap glanced up and down the stripper pole that was secured in the middle of the room. He could only imagine how it played a part in Cash and Jasmin conceiving their baby.

"Like I was saying," Trap returned to the subject, "this Olivia..." he was shaking his head unsure about how to continue the conversation.

"My nigga, if we keep moving like we been moving, ain't no tellin' how things may play out. At least this way we are lowering the risk of one of our hubs getting raided. Then what?"

Trap looked at his friend and smiled. He didn't want to believe it at first, but the evidence was getting stronger and stronger.

"Man, what the fuck you smiling for?"

"You hittin' that, ain't you?"

Cash threw his head back and laughed. "Fool, you done lost

your mind."

"Nawl, nigga, I ain't seen a woman have you off your square like this in a long-time pimp. You better not let J find out, cause she gone cut your dick off," Trap laughed

"Nigga, ain't shit going on between me and shorty, but I want you to take me serious on this one family."

Trap looked off in deep thought before replying. "Let me get back to you on this one then, my nigga, cause I can't just up and agree to something like this without first giving it some thought."

Cash looked at him confused. He knew the idea was a great idea. An opportunity had presented itself for them to move in a different direction. Moreless, Trap was his number one man, and if he needed more time to think it over, then so be it.

"Take all the time you need, my nigga," he told him standing up to shake his hand. They embraced for a brief hug before Cash said, "Now, come over here so I can beat your ass in some pool."

They both walked over to the pool stick rack and grabbed a stick.

"Man, whatever you say pinky."

CHAPTER 12

ALPHA MALE

"Push, baby, push!" Cash coached her.

"Ahhhhhhh!" Jasmin screamed in return. She was on the verge of passing out as she tried repeatedly to push baby Legacy out her vagina. She secretly told herself that if she made it through this child's birth, there would not be another.

"Come on baby, you are doing just fine." He was filled with joy as he watched nature take its course. Any minute now he would be holding his most prized possession and couldn't wait.

"Give me one more push, Mrs. Lewis," the doctor urged, standing between her legs ready to catch their baby.

She no longer had the moniker, Jasmin Myers either. For now on, she would be referred to as Jasmin Lewis. After Cash explained to her why they couldn't get legally married in the U.S., she took it upon herself to go down to the Social Security Office and have her name changed herself. Since Cash was supposed to be deceased, he knew if they tried to get married it would reveal that he is still alive. He knew it would be a mistake that would cost them in the long run, and since there was no room for error they made the decision not to. Jasmin knew he was right, however, she was willing to take matters into her own hands to get what she wanted; and that was to have his last name before she brought their child into this world.

For about another 3 minutes, she panted exhaustively before giving-in and pushing with all her might. She knew sooner or later it would all be over with, so she tried her best to push Legacy out her womb. The way she was feeling, she figured she'd either be dead, or if she was lucky enough, the mother of a pretty little girl. Both results seemed to be a relief she could deal with to avoid the constant pain she was enduring. So, as she looked into the eyes of the only man she had ever loved, appreciating all his love and support, she gave it one last push.

"Eeeeeeh," she shrieked, clamping down on his hand like a crab trying to evade capture. Sweat was pouring down her face by the pint. Everything was becoming blurry as the sweat ran into her eyes. As the pain began to subside, joy filled her heart when she heard her baby crying. Cash was no longer by her side. He was too busy enjoying the presence of their new tangible connection. When the doctor placed bloody Legacy in his hands, he walked back over to Jasmin and gently laid their creation in her arms. She was tired but had more than enough energy to hold her baby. Baby Legacy was her signature forever etched into Cash's heart. Their union as a family had been solidified. Hopefully, now since he witnessed the magic they could make together, she expected him to make the right choice for their family and leave the drug dealing business alone. He promised her a long time ago he would once they were financially stable, so she planned on making him live up to that promise.

"You did good sweetheart, you did real good," he whispered to her, bending down and kissing her glossy forehead.

She smiled at his show of affection, and replied, "No honey, we did good."

***

"I'm in," Trap announced after giving the idea to bring Olivia to their table a second thought. "I thought about it my nigga, and you're right. We gotta stay ten steps ahead of the competition, so since you've been driving this whip carefully, fuck it! I'm gonna continue ridin' in it with you cuzzo."

Cash smiled.

"Say no more my nigga." He hung up the phone and called Olivia.

Waiting for her to pick up, he silently congratulated himself on his management skills. He had it all planned out perfectly. With Olivia's resources, and their connections to an unlimited supply of cocaine, they were destined for greatness. It hadn't even been two years since that deadly assault took place on him and his brother, and now he was about to finally get the revenge he set out to get. Everything was about to fall into place. The look in his little girl's eyes told him that it was time to put old beefs to rest in the graveyard, and that's exactly what he planned on doing.

But first, he had to make sure the organization he worked so hard to build, would forever be in good hands. Trap didn't know it yet, but he would one day oversee their entire empire. He had his mind made up the moment he saw how perfect him, Jasmin, and their daughter looked together. He had a family to be responsible for, and he knew, remaining in the deadly world of the drug trade would not be conducive to the welfare of what he loved most. The mere fact that he was making a departure from the criminal world shouldn't be too surprising to Trap. After all, if it wasn't for Money beating Latina half to death, he would've already been out of the dope game. The madness that caused him to go even further in it was about to come to an end, and he was relieved.

"Hola, Papi," Olivia answered seductively.

"Como estas, senorita," he replied, "check it out, everything is good on my end, so go ahead and start making those preparations."

"Okay then, Papi, hasta luego."

"Adios."

***

Mercedees was so embarrassed after catching Darryl out with another man. He had completely humiliated her. There was no way in hell she was going to give him the time of day after something like that. Darryl was bisexual. He apparently liked the same thing she liked, and that was dick. The picture had been painted vividly for her when she caught him with his head in another man's lap. The thought of him turned her stomach sour and it continued to make her sick. She wasn't so sure if she was going to recover or not. If it wasn't for her three bodyguards rushing over and helping, she didn't know how things would've turned out. Whoever was in the passenger side of his car, overstepped his boundary by laying his hands on her. She didn't feel a bit of sympathy for him as her three goons went to work.

Out of nowhere, two of them rushed over and grabbed the unknown man, preventing him from taking ahold of her. The other one pointed his gun at Darryl, putting the fear of God in him. After seeing him bitch-up, Mercedees ran over and finished her assault. For a while, he just took it, allowing her to release her anger and frustration out on him. But when he noticed she had no intention on stopping anytime soon, he took off running. She tried chasing after him, but the bodyguard with the gun stopped her.

She watched as onlookers surrounded them with their phones out. She knew if they didn't get out of there fast, the whole situation would go viral in a matter of minutes. So, she ran over to where the other two were busy beating their latest victim and screamed, "Stop before y'all kill him!"

At the sound of her voice, TP and Juvi stopped, looking around at the audience they had attracted. They pulled out their weapons and told everyone to get back into their cars.

No one thought to contest the demands as they immediately dispersed. They had gotten enough footage to please their followers and didn't see any reason to jeopardize their life for anymore.

Mercedees ordered her bodyguards to leave, then she rushed to her car and did the same. It had been one of her worst nights, and she regretted the day she met Darryl.

As she combed her hair, she laughed to herself as she thought about that night. Her three heroes were something else. In the midst of all the mayhem, she forgot about the security detail that was assigned to watch her back. She wasn't expecting for them to show up, but they did, and she was grateful. They had her back and she appreciated them. Posing in her vanity mirror, she blew herself a kiss, pleased with her look. She was gorgeous, and she knew if Darryl wanted him some dick instead of what she had to offer, then so be it, but she'd be damned if she crossed the yellow brick road with him and pursued another woman. Although she had friends that were gay, that was by far, not her style, and she was going to keep it that way.

"Bitch, is you gone stay in there all day or what?" She heard her roommate shout from the other side of the door.

"Girl, here I come, damn!" She shot back.

Her and two of her girlfriends had plans on going out to the club with a couple of guys, and she was holding them up. She took it upon herself to invite her bodyguards out since they helped her with the whole Darryl situation. She figured the least she could do was treat them to a good time. When she introduced them to her roommates a few days later, the rest was history. Her friends couldn't get enough of the gangsters who came to her rescue. They enjoyed their company and couldn't wait for the next opportunity to be around them. Mercedees was intentionally holding the process up so she could let her friends know who was in charge. Although she felt like they were all equals at the end of the day, she wanted them to know that the show didn't start until she was ready.

After exiting the bathroom, she walked over to her bed and grabbed her Burberry Peyton Cross body bag. She did a quick full body check in the wall mirror to make sure her shit was tight, then she walked over to the door and opened it.

"Damn!" She complained, looking at her friends who were growing impatient by the minute. "Y'all bitches act like y'all ain't never been nowhere."

They scoffed at her statement but didn't reply. They knew there was some truth to it, being how they were both from small towns, but never would admit it. She was the baddest bitch of them all and they wouldn't dare try to compare themselves to her. They envied her, but praised the ground she walked on. She was of another breed and they knew it, but she allowed them the opportunity to be in her presence, so that was enough for them to stay by her side.

"Listen," she said, making sure she had their attention, "TP's mine, so stay away from him, alright?"

They both nodded, agreeing that she got first pick. As she led them down the hall, she slid her shades on her face, and thought to herself, "Now, that's a bad bitch!"

***

"I want all of y'all to understand that this move is what's best for all of us. I don't need for anyone to question it, so just be on point and stay focused," Trap instructed everyone as they attentively listened. He glanced over at Olivia and said, "Olivia is going to make sure that all the packages are accurately weighed and shipped, but each one of y'all will have to send her one of these before you receive a shipment."

He snapped his finger at Olivia, and she stepped forward, passing each one of them a shipment order form."

"Does everyone understand?"

Smoke, Twan, JJ, and Outkast, all nodded in unison. They understood exactly what was going on. They were about to turn their East Coast enterprise into a national network and become legends.

They all stood around looking at the order forms she'd just given them. The system Trap designed for them to move the cocaine undetected was brilliant. Only a genius could be so creative and innovative, and they silently applauded him for taking the dope game to a new level.

They were beginning to enjoy their executive meetings with him. In every meeting he offered something new to add to their organization for it to grow and be the best. As they stood there waiting to be dismissed, he read all of their faces. He knew his orders were received unobjectively. For the past hour, he had broken down to them, step-by-step, how things were to be handled. Mistakes would not be tolerated. Everybody had a part to play including him. The time to advance themselves was now, not later. There was plenty of money to be made, and more than enough to go around. A greedy heart would be consumed and annihilated by the members of their organization if need be. Big I's and little u's were only considered vowels, and not factors in what they had worked so hard to establish. Trap wouldn't allow it, and neither would Cash.

Soon, the time would come for Cash to reveal himself to his fellow members. Playing the backfield was only supposed to be temporary until they got their revenge, eliminating their biggest threat. Although Cash and Olivia stayed in constant communication with each other, the rest of them hadn't even known he was still alive, or even existed. Some people, who were still operating for them in Bibb County, were aware of his survival. However, they vowed to never say a word about it. A lot of the dope being distributed throughout Georgia touched their hands, and as long as they continued to eat, they wouldn't dare cut off the hand that fed them.

"One more thing," he said, almost forgetting another important part of their meeting, "Olivia will be hiring all of you a financial adviser. The way you spend your money is very important, and we," he paused, gesturing with his hands as if to say all of us, "need to make sure that nobody throws up any red flags."

When they all nodded in agreement, he continued.

"Now, y'all be easy, and I'll see y all later."

On that note, everyone except Olivia and Trap, got into their newly bought foreign cars and left. The whole crew had attained a level of success beyond their dreams, and even though they felt like they owed it all to Trap, in all actuality, they owed it to Cash.

"I'll be down there next week to view the process if you don't mind," he informed her, walking over to his Lambo.

She wasn't feeling his attitude. She followed Cash's instructions about letting Trap do all the talking, but she wasn't about to keep putting up with his stank attitude.

"What is the problem here?" She asked, confused as she paced behind him.

He turned around to address her. "Check it out ma," he said, walking up to her and closing the space between them to about a foot. "There is no problem here. I'm just meeting you, and since this is business, I am serious about maintaining this business. Do you understand?"

She was taken aback by his straight forwardness. His honesty was blunt and tasteless, but yet understanding. Looking into his eyes, she knew without a shadow of a doubt, he meant every word. It was all business to him, and she understood that, but the fact that he was towering over her Nicki Minaj frame, smelling so good, didn't help the situation at all. Taking in his scent a little more, her look of distaste slowly began to turn into a look of admiration. He was a man of power, and she had just realized it. There was no coincidence that him and Cash were so close. Birds of a feather flocked together, and they were definitely from the same breed. As she continued to take in his presence, feeling the moisture begin to build between her legs, she took a deep breath. The confidence in his swag, along with his handsome features was turning her on. That's moment she realized she was in the presence of an Alpha.

Then, just when she thought things were about to change for the both of them, he spoke up, taking her out of her daze.

"Are we clear?" He asked, completely unaware of her attraction to him.

"Crystal!" she replied, getting a grip on herself.

Trap turned around and walked to his car. Getting in and pulling off, Olivia wasn't surprised by his dismissal.

"Whoah!" she sighed, fanning herself as she walked over to her Lexus Coupe and got in. Revving up the engine, she singed Salt-N-Pepa's, "What a man, what a man, what a man, what a mighty good man!"

CHAPTER 13

SUCCESS

"Ugh!" Tameka panted as she gasped for air.

The sex was overwhelmingly good. Her nails dug deeper into his back as he drove deeper into her womb. Their bodies laid locked together in missionary as they rode the wave of love. The sweat from hours of love making had their naked bodies glistening in the night.

Trap held her hands above her head, their fingers entwined, as he drove deeper and deeper into her soul. It was an intense moment for the two new lovebirds. You would have thought they were trying to make a baby the way they were going at it. She sucked on his bottom lip while he kissed the top of her's. Saliva was being shared uncontrollably as they allowed their emotions to take over.

"Ahhhhh!" she screamed, releasing her thick cream all over his fat dick. He was expanding her walls with every stroke. He groaned at the feel of her pussy tightening around his member. She constantly trembled and he knew why; the sex was amazing.

As their eyes met, lust being the only emotion they could interpret, she whispered to him what she thought would complete the moment.

"Oooooh...I love you," she cried, her heart speaking louder than the Tyrese track playing in the background.

"I love..." he mumbled, not getting a chance to complete his sentence as his tongue dived back into her mouth. Their tongues wrestled while their bodies danced to their own soul music.

"Mhmmmm..." she moaned, not knowing if her body could handle another orgasm. She started shaking as he thrust his hips forward between her chocolate thighs.

"Fuck!" he shouted, releasing the little bit of sperm left his worn-out testicles could produce. He was so tired he just laid down on top of her with his semi-limp dick resting inside her warm enclosure. They kissed for a little while before giving their bodies time to rest. Love had taken over their relationship. It was not something they had planned, but it was bliss. They made each other happy, relatives or not, that didn't matter anymore. If anybody had a problem with it, so be it. They had only one life to live, and they'd be damned if they let others decide what was best for them.

When he finally conjured up enough energy to roll over, not wanting to smoother her with his long frame, he did. Tameka's body, on the other hand, remained sprawled out still shuddering from the nerves in her vagina reacting to him sliding out of her.

***

She was on the verge of losing her composure as she stood there sizing up the latest perpetrator to cross her path.

The agent questioning the dealer was too soft for her liking. For what seemed like hours, Agent Bradley watched from behind the tinted glass of the interrogation room, the Agent beat around the bush. This wasn't what she signed up for. Pussy footing around with criminals was not her thing. She was direct and straight forward. Either you talked willingly, or we beat you until you decided to tell it all. The ass kicking part wasn't really apart of her interrogation training, but she didn't care. She had earned her right to violate a few Constitutional rights here or there. The Federal Government would ensure that she kept her job if a Civil Complaint were to just pop up on her. They had her back, and she knew it. So, with that in mind, she did whatever it was she knew she could get away with.

"Got damn, Tom!" she stressed to her boss, Assistant Director Tom Beddingfield. "Where in the fuck did you get this wimp?" Tom, with his arms crossed and eyebrow raised, turned his head towards her and said, "Do you think you can do a better job without over doing it?"

It was a question she knew she couldn't answer. From the moment they brought the dread headed trafficker into the federal building, she wanted to pull him into one of their observation rooms, and treat him like a bitch, slapping him around and telling him how she was going to lock his mother, grandmother, and great-grandmother up.

She nervously chewed away at her fingernails as the thought of rushing in there and kicking his chair from up under him crossed her mind. She had done it so many times before, she knew right away she would get the response she was looking for. She glanced out the corner of her eye and noticed her boss was still waiting for an answer.

Deep down inside, he knew she could get it done, however, with the Regional Director on his ass about her long list of complaints, he wasn't willing to throw her back in the ring. She was a hot head. The fact that a woman of her size and race could be so damn aggressive was beyond him. At times, he encouraged her behavior, because it kept the heat off of him. White male agents were always considered the bad guys, and he didn't like that stereotype. So, he was kind of glad that he could finally pass the torch down to a minority.

"I will not put my hands on him Tom, I swear," she lied, knowing she mastered the art of physical abuse. Despite the camera being on and her boss standing right there, she knew exactly how to get around the eyes of the law.

When he gave her a slight nod, off she went.

As she snatched the door open to the interrogation room, the occupants' eyeballs darted over towards her way. The agent questioning the suspect shook his head. He knew from the stories over at the academy how vicious Veronica Bradley could be.

"Out!" she ordered, barely having the authority to demand such a request.

"Well, I tried to help you my friend," the agent warned the antsy drug dealer as he walked out of the room, not even bothering to address his fellow agent. The look in her eyes told him everything he needed to know about what was about to transpire.

"Man, I want a lawyer," the trafficker announced, looking at her as If she would be the one to find an attorney.

She broke out in a heavy laugh as if she was interrogating Mike Epps. Him asking for a lawyer didn't faze her. She was determined to get what she wanted, no matter how bad he wanted to exercise his Sixth Amendment.

She slowly walked around the room, circling around her prey like a shark in the ocean. He was her dinner and didn't even know it.

"Soooooo," she began, stretching the 'so' out longer than necessary. "You want an attorney. I think we can do that." She was standing behind him now, bent down over his shoulder while he continued looking straight ahead.

"What are you going to give me in return?" she whispered in his ear.

Even though he was wearing Burberry Cologne, and the smell of his dreads were fresh, she could still smell pussy all over him.

"Bitch, I ain't giving you...ahhhh!" he hollered, the feeling of her pulling one of his dreads sent a sharp pain down his back. "Oooooh, what's wrong?" she cooed, standing between him and the tinted glass. The camera was angled down in front of him where her hand couldn't be seen as it creeped around the back of his head.

"Listen, dummy!" she growled into his ear, five dreads in her hand now instead of one. "You are looking at a mandatory minimum of fifteen years for those sixteen bricks we got out of your vehicle. So, you can play hardball all you want, but if you don't tell me something, and I mean fast, I'm gonna start pulling some of these dumb ass dreads out of the back of your head until you look maimed."

"Ssssss," he hissed, the pain soaring throughout his body. His cuffs jangled as he fought to break them loose from the hook that had him secured to the desk.

She slowly began pulling on the dreads along the back of his hairline. His head was rising by the second as she continued pulling, her face next to his, awaiting a response.

When his mouth opened to speak, so did her's, mocking him as if she knew it would come out sooner or later.

"Cast," he replied, finally giving up. "I got the shit from my nigga Outcast."

She let go of his dreads and smiled, "Now was that so hard?" She asked before walking to the door and exiting the room.

When she returned to the room parallel to the interrogation room, she looked over at her boss who a\was standing next to the rookie agent and asked, "What's my time?"

Tom looked at his stopwatch and said, "Not a new record sweetheart." He had begun timing her the moment she stepped in the room. It had become a tradition for them.

"Arghhh!" she shouted before storming off.

***

"You've come a long way my friend," Felix commented. "To success!" He raised a glass filled with some of the finest champagne in the air end waited for Cash to join him in a toast.

"To success!" he cheerfully added, clearly pleased by Felix's description of where they were in life. They were definitely successful. From growing up in the gang infested streets of Macon, Georgia, to sipping Perignon Spucca on an island, he would have to agree he was successful.

Before having a chance to contact The Ghost about arranging a meeting to discuss their future business plans, Felix contacted him. He was so pleased with Cash's, he decided to invite him and his family out to his private island in the Gulf of California. The narrow stretch of ocean water that filtered into Mexico was the perfect place for them to relax. In the daytime, the sunny sky above made everything bright enough to bring the life out of everyone who enjoyed the island's active atmosphere. While at night, the cool weather allowed them to unwind and embrace its serene setting.

When a volleyball rolled over towards their area, disrupting their conversation, Cash grabbed it and tossed it back over to where Jasmin and Shay were playing Felix's wife and daughter in a game of volleyball. He smiled as Jasmin retrieved the ball and gave him a wink. She had picked up a few pounds after giving birth to their daughter Legacy, but he enjoyed watching it bounce up and down as she jogged back over to where they were competing. They were happily enjoying the moment and he couldn't blame them.

At first, Jasmin was a little reluctant about leaving her new-born at home, but after Ms. Tina insisted that she would be in good hands. She asked Shay to come along for the trip since they had become good friends over the years despite the friendship Shay still held with Peaches. The minute their beef was squashed at Peaches graduation, Shay told herself that she would no longer get in-between the two hearts that, for a while, fought over Cash. He had been the common denominator in their feud and they hated each other because of him. Although Peaches still had a piece of his heart wrapped around her neck, the woman who rightly deserved his love, wholeheartedly had it.

After watching them return to their game, he walked back over to where Felix was seated.

"They look like they're enjoying themselves over there," Felix stated.

"They are," Cash said in return, taking his seat in the bench chair next to Felix, "How long have you owned this place?"

"For about 2 years," he replied, snapping his fingers for one of his bodyguards to come over. A stocky Mexican in a suit approached the men with ease as he waited for his boss to speak.

"Have Maria bring our food out here, Juan. I think today would be a nice day to eat out on the beach. What do you say?" He looked over at Cash.

"I think that's a great idea," he agreed, stretching his legs out as he leaned back in his chair.

Juan nodded and took off, speaking in Spanish to two other bodyguards before ducking off into a path surrounded by mango trees. There was a total of twenty bodyguards left standing nearby. The security was necessary, Felix was one of the most powerful men in Mexico, and he needed to be always protected.

"There is nothing more a man could ask for, eh?" Felix peered over at him expecting for him to agree.

That's when Cash remembered the important matter he had to discuss with the drug lord. "Well, on that note," he began, sitting up and facing him, "I do need your help on something that I think would be beneficial to the both of us."

"Then speak on it my friend," he told him, his face not displaying any emotion as he watched his wife spike the ball down for a point.

Cash glanced over to where his attention was focused, then looked back. "I need to eliminate a threat to our organization," he stated plainly.

Felix didn't know if he was referring to the organization he had in the States, or the organization he had with him. Either way, a threat regarding Cash was in-fact a threat to him, so he urged him to continue.

"And?"

"Well, the Zeta Cartel. I need to destroy their entire empire, but I cannot do it with just the resources I have in the States. I am gonna need your help on this."

Felix smirked at his proposition, turning his head to look him in his eyes. "Is this to avenge your brother's death?"

Cash's heart skipped a beat at the mention of his deceased sibling. 'How did he know?' he thought to himself. He hesitated before responding.

"Yes," he decided to answer truthfully.

The cat was out the bag. Felix was smart and Cash acknowledged that, but how could he know about something so secretive?

"You seem surprised," Felix observed, noticing his uneasiness.

"Well don't be. I heard about the two brothers who were allegedly killed in Central Georgia not too long ago," he said, putting emphasis on the allege.

"I've done my research on you Mr. Lewis. Just think about who brought you to me?"

"Jose," he barely whispered.

He had forgotten all about his pal Jose. He didn't even think he knew about the assassination attempt on his life. It was something that happened in Georgia, not Florida, however, the streets did have ways of carrying gossip.

Felix had no clue that the Zeta's were responsible for Money's death. It was Cash who had unknowingly informed him. Only after hearing him say he wanted to destroy the Zetas did he actually know who killed his brother. It was not the kind of song he expected to hear, but still, it was music to his ears.

"So," Felix began, "you want my help to take out the Zeta's." He stroked his neatly trimmed goatee while he pondered the thought, already knowing his answer. "How do you plan on doing this?"

Cash smiled once he knew he was all in. "Well, that's easy," he said, looking over at the girls as they repeatedly jumped up and down to keep the ball in the air.

"I know their family."

***

"Roger that, Alpha One. We have a visual on the suspect," Agent Bradley heard one of the team leaders radio-in.

"Okay, Delta," she radioed back, "keep your eyes on him and don't let him out of your sight."

"Copy, out!"

"Charlie team, come in," she called over the radio.

"Go ahead for Charlie team."

"If the suspect gets on the interstate, take over for Delta in pursuit. Copy?"

"Charlie team, copy!"

Agent Bradley sped through traffic as she directed the teams surveilling Outcast. The information she had received from the trafficker led her to believe that this Outcast guy was a key element to the drug trade in Savannah. This Outcast guy could potentially be the link she needed to get a step further towards catching Trap. So far, though, he was just leading them around town on a bunch of errands.

Earlier, he made a stop at the Bank of America on McKinley Street, to make either a deposit, or a withdrawal. That, she didn't know. There was no confirmation from the surveillance team closest to him on whether he did or not, because they saw him carry the same bag in-and-out of the bank. From there, he went to a bunch of different utility companies and paid some bills. Now, he was riding around shopping.

She noticed, for someone to be so young, he managed a lot of responsibilities. Bank accounts. Utility bills. There was something strange about this case that she just couldn't get a grip on, but she was determined to figure it out. The car he was driving, a Nissan Altima, was far from the average brick mover's image. When the dread headed trafficker informed her that he had gotten all sixteen keys from this guy, she expected to see someone who flaunted a luxurious lifestyle. This kid they were watching, was not the fly-guy drug dealer she was expecting. He moved like an average civilian.

The thought began to cross her mind that maybe she was being sent out on a wild goose chase. She remembered making herself perfectly clear to Dread that if he lied to her about anything, their deal was off. He would not receive anything in exchange for his halfway cooperation, but instead, be indicted and prosecuted to the full extent of the law. She would personally see to it that he received every punishment allowed for wasting her time.

"Delta to Alpha, do you have a copy?"

"Alpha here, copy," she replied with haste.

"Suspect just pulled into a parking garage downtown on

Mulberry Street, copy?"

"Copy that, Delta. Do not pursue suspect into the garage. Park outside and wait on me." She looked at her watch and said, "I'll be there in 2 mics Delta, copy?"

"Delta, copy out."

She tossed the radio over onto the passenger seat and made a wide illegal u-turn, barely missing a parked van. She pressed down on the accelerator as she weaved left and right throw traffic. She wasn't sure if him going into the parking garage would lead to anything, but she wasn't going to chance missing out on it. She rolled down the window, allowing the cool breeze to enter the car as she drove 70 miles per hour in a 45-mile zone. Peering into the rearview mirror she saw the tiredness behind her eyes. To be so young, she looked ten years her senior. She wouldn't allow Maybelline to cover up the hard work and many hours she'd put in on this case. It was a gift to her brother and all the family members who had lost a loved one to the drug game. Her ambitious attitude towards removing all drug dealing scum from the face of the earth was damn near maniacal. Who needed sleep or rest when there was a job to do? At least that's how she felt about it.

**

Mercedees laughed at how silly TP was acting. He was making fun of Darryl and his gay lover.

"Oh, no you didn't just hit my man miss thang," he joked, rolling his head and snapping his finger.

"Boy you need to stop," she laughed, "it wasn't like that." "Oh, yes it was honey," he continued.

They were walking through downtown Atlanta taking in the rapid nightlife. She was impressed by his vocabulary. His choice of words during their conversation was well above any street thug she had ever met. He articulated himself nicely, and she liked that a lot. His handsome features made him easy on the eyes, but his smile is what drew her in the most. He was a well-kept young man, and that was a plus in her book. There were things about him she would have never guessed.

"I like this little piece you put together tonight," he said, complimenting her on her outfit.

"It's cute ain't it," she agreed, stopping to give him a pose of her curves in her Jason Wu thigh high dress. The Just Fab Fur Boots she was rocking complemented her milk chocolate legs and matched her Diane Von Furstenberg Fur Coat. She was trying to show him her sense of style so he would see that she was different from her friends.

He licked his lips as he checked her out. "Yeah ma, you're beautiful."

She knew his words were genuine by the tone in his voice. The look in his eyes let her know that he was feeling her. When she noticed his penetrating eyes were all over her body, she blushed.

"Thank you, you're not too bad yourself."

Even though she was dressed to impress, she wore her hair pretty basic, hot combing it so he could see that she had naturally long hair. She was a beautiful girl, but to hear someone else tell her, made her feel good. The years her brothers sheltered her, keeping her in the house away from all the troubled boys in their neighborhood deprived her of receiving compliments like the one he just gave her. She knew at the end of the day they were just being overprotective.

As they continued walking and talking, TP's hand slightly brushed against her's. The touch was sweat and innocent, but did something to the both of them, so she decided to act on her emotions the next time his hand swung close to her's, she deliberately pushed her's out a little further so they could meet. When they did, like clockwork they began swinging pendulously together. Her fingers locked-in with his as their arms swung together. It was elementary, but romantic. Harmless, but sexually arousing. Wrong, but so right. They walked hand-and-hand as if they were boyfriend and girlfriend.

It was love in the making, and both of them was secretly hoping the happiness they were feeling would last forever.

CHAPTER 14

NYMPHO

Agent Bradley and her team of agents, along with a few U.S. Marshal's, patiently waited for their suspect to emerge from the parking garage. There was only one way in and one way out. On foot, or in a vehicle, either way, they had the perimeter surrounded so he would not get away. There were eyes staring through an unknown amount of binoculars, looking-in from all directions. They were on a high priority assignment, and that meant for everyone being alert, "Bravo to Alpha, copy?"

Silence

"Repeat, Bravo to Alpha come in, copy?" Still no response. Bravo, Charlie, and Delta all tried to radio in to their operation leader, but there was no response. Agent Bradley had went completely off the grid. She had committed what they called in the academy a grave sin. If we were still in the Draconian era, she would've been executed for her unacceptable wrongdoing. After countless weeks of fighting the urge, her body finally gave in to the desire that continuously haunted her. No, she would not be able to come back from this weakness that was frowned upon by all law enforcement agencies across the globe. She was the victim and the victimizer. The cause and the effect. The problem and the answer. She was asleep.

The ominous warning of long days and short nights besieged her, but she failed to acknowledge it. She was tired. Her body could not take it anymore. The comfortable leather seat she was sitting in had taken ahold of her, leading her down the path to Sandman's land. The long river of drool, connecting her mouth to her chin displayed just how long she'd been out.

She stirred a little, probably not from the dream she was lost in, but the constant radio chatter. Her coworkers were trying to understand what was going on with her. Just when everyone thought she was down for the count, the bell dinged.

Knock! Knock! Knock!

"Okay, Michael, I swear!" she shouted erratically, awakening from her dream, her brother's death obviously still haunting her.

The agent who volunteered to go check on her was impatiently standing outside her door. He didn't expect to catch her sleeping on the job, but the evidence was clear. Police scanner in one hand, binoculars in the other. She was out like a light.

Noticing the rookie standing outside her door, she tried regaining her composure. She wiped the Nile River away from her chin and sat up straight. She was embarrassed and ashamed for getting caught with her pants down. For the next couple of weeks, she could imagine how she would be the talk of the Bureau. She would be the joke that everybody thought was funny. She hated herself for becoming so vulnerable during such an important time.

"Agent Bradley, open the door!" Now, he was the one giving her orders.

As she opened the door, preferring rather to go find a rock to hide under, she said, "I'm awake agent-"

"He's already gone," he cut her off, "open the door so I can get in." He ran around to the passenger side and got in.

She started the car as he got in, and asked, "How long has he been gone?"

"Long enough for you to take a nap," he thought to himself, not wanting to get her started. "Only a few minutes. Bravo, Charlie, and Delta are all in pursuit. Bravo leader has temporarily taken over command."

That little bit of information made her cringe. This was her operation, and she didn't appreciate how someone other than herself was calling the shots. Although she felt misplaced, she was glad it hadn't turned out worst for her. Sleeping during surveillance got you reprimanded. So, when he used the word temporarily to describe the update, that let her know; she was still in the fight.

"Bravo team, copy?" she spoke into the radio.

"This is Bravo, copy."

"Alpha team here, Bravo. Let me get an ETA and a status check, copy?"

"Welcome back Alpha. We are about ten minutes out, heading north on I-95. Suspect is now driving a white Box-truck truck labeled Bare Essentials, and suspect is still solo, copy?"

"Copy that Bravo, Alpha team in route."

"Copy that Alpha!"

She gritted her teeth out of frustration. She had missed something important, and it didn't sit well with her.

"Bare Essentials," she said to herself, repeating the name stenciled on the side of the truck. 'Was he working?' she thought. She wasn't familiar with the company, but believed something smelled fishy. She wasn't sure whether it was her or the situation.

After all, she hadn't bathed in two days.

She was back to her usual, speeding beyond the limit as she turned a corner doing around 50 mph. The ramp to get on the interstate was up ahead, so she swerved over into the right-hand lane in order to merge onto the highway. Her passenger was holding on for his life. He had no clue race car driving was a part of their training. Clearly, Agent Bradley played by her own rules. As he sat back in his seat, bracing himself against the door and her seat, he looked over at her, and thought to himself, "And I'm the one supposed to be the Rookie.

Tameka brushed her nose up against Trap's, licking his lips as if she was a cat trying to wake her master.

He stirred a little from her call but didn't awake. He was tired. Tired from running the streets and exhausted from making love. His body was trying to get some well needed rest while it had the chance, but Tameka just wouldn't allow it.

Repositioning herself, she slid her thick chocolate leg over his body, cocking it to a 45-degree angle. Her naked body laid halfway over his as she pulled the silk sheets over the both of them to keep them warm. They had lit a fire between them hours ago and she didn't want it to go out. She braced herself, leaning on his chest so she could watch him sleep. Tremors ran through her body all the way up to her hungry clit as she continued licking his brown smooth lips. She wanted to stick her tongue in his mouth and finish where they'd left off. She was almost sure they had already did the R. Kelly and went half in on a baby. Every milligram of sperm he had produced was either swirling around in her stomach, or was making its way through her fallopian tubes. She had sucked and fucked him dry, and he enjoyed every bit of it.

She looked over towards her nightstand when she saw his phone come to life. It was too late for someone to be calling him, so she ignored it, not even bothering to wake him. Trap had did so much for everyone else, she figured it was time for someone to finally do something for him.

She slowly lifted herself up, getting on all fours, making sure not to wake him just yet. She was positioned right over him, the look in her lustful eyes revealing how bad she wanted to pounce on her prey. Instead, she slithered her way down his body, head completely under the sheets as she searched for what kept her awake.

Once she found it, like a pro with no hands, she placed it in her mouth. Her tongue lifted the head of it up, awakening his snake, and guiding it into her warm mouth.

"Mhmmmmmm," she moaned, enjoying the feeling of it growing inside her mouth. She soft stroked it until it was hard enough to deep throat.

When Trap finally awoke, he pulled the sheets back and watched as her head bobbed up-and-down his member. She was too much for him. This would be their fourth time making love and he didn't know how he could keep-on going. The only thing that could explain her behavior was, nympho.

***

"Got damn!" Cash stressed under his breath, placing his phone in his pocket. "Where the fuck is he at?"

He was about to board a helicopter but needed to run a few things by his best friend first. The loud propellers were barely giving him enough room to hear Trap's answering machine pick up.

After speaking with Felix about seeking revenge on Manny, Negro, and Migo, everything was a go. They were going to hit the Zetas tonight. Felix knew about most of their territories in Mexico, but he didn't have any knowledge as to their whereabouts in the States. Turns out, Manny was not just a member of the cartel, he was the leader. Cash was shocked by this information. All this time he thought they were just some pawns in a game they had no real control over. To hear that he was in bed with the devil himself, further convinced him that they needed to be destroyed. It seemed, Felix was more excited about it than he was. He had lost many men in the war against his rival and couldn't wait for the opportunity to cut the head off of the snake that's been spewing its venom throughout Mexico. Manny had killed one of his brothers, and in exchange, Felix delivered the large amount of bodies Cash seen in the U.S. Today. It was a war that costed many their lives, but would shortly come to an end.

"Oye, Cash!" Juan yelled from the awaiting chopper.

When he turned around, he saw Juan waving for him to come on. He was supposed to show him where all of them lived and go from there. The plan was to hit all of their residences at once, giving them no time to alert each other about the attacks. With Felix already having people on the U.S. side of the border, it would be fairly easy for them to put together a multiple assault team. Cash also had ten of his own men in route to Houston to meet up with the five he already had there.

Unbeknownst to Manny, he had been watching them for the past six months. He knew where all of their stash houses were in the States, and where all of them lived. He had properly planned for this day, looking forward to the moment he could look Migo in his eyes as he sent a bullet through his skull. He knew Migo had no control over what Money did, or the fact that Manny issued the kill order. However, these were the circumstances they lived bye. You either kill or be killed. He knew if he allowed Migo to live past the death of his two uncles, it would come back to haunt him. The sinister look in his eyes the day he had his so-called Frenemies executed kept passing through his mind. It was the look of the devil. His anger had reached a boiling point, causing him to go temporarily insane. Cash would not allow that kind of maliciousness to take place against the people he loved. So, there was only one thing to do, kill Migo and his uncles.

"We're pulling in people from Brownsville, Laredo and Del Rio," Juan informed him as he reached down to pull him onto the chopper.

"Everyone will be in place when we get there. My men have orders to meet your men in Houston."

Cash nodded.

Nothing else needed to be said. He sat down in a seat and buckled up. He glanced around at the Mexicans who would accompany him on this mission. They all had the look of determination written on their faces as if they had also lost some family in the war. Dressed in all black military gear, they held on as the helicopter made its departure from the ground. This was Cash's first time in a helicopter, and probably would be his last. The feeling in his stomach made him second guess not taking a plane back with the girls, but that was not an option. They had to act order to take out the drug lords and stop the five-year long war.

***

"He's leaving the house now Alpha. What do you want us to do?"

Agent Bradley had been watching it all take place but knew better than to jump the gun.

"Do not engage guys until we know what's going on," she instructed them, attentively watching as Outcast suddenly reappeared from behind the Box-truck.

After sitting in the driveway for almost two hours, Outcast hopped in the Box-truck and pulled off. He had no clue that the federal government had followed him all the way to Fayetteville, North Carolina.

Agent Bradley and her fellow agents got into position as he begun to move. Bravo was parked five houses down from the house, while Charlie and Delta sat on adjacent streets. Alpha, on the other hand, remained mobile.

Agent Bradley decided to park her car on the other end of the street where it would be out of view to any wondering eyes. She told the rookie to stay in the car while she posted-up on foot. Unable to stay still, she ended up making her way towards the house across the street. Binoculars in hand, she watched as Outcast, and another guy unloaded boxes from the back of the truck. She didn't have the best view, but she was still able to make-out what was transpiring behind the vehicle.

"Delta team, you copy?" she called over the radio. She used a spot behind the neighbor's house to conduct her surveillance.

"Delta team here, copy."

"Have Fayetteville PD stop that truck for us and question the driver."

"Copy, Delta out!"

Agent Bradley was onto something, and she believed it was something big. After running the tag on the box-truck, it came back that the truck belonged to a Ms. Olivia Mendez, the owner of Bare Essentials Cosmetics. The company, headquartered out of Florida, and was one of the only cosmetics lines that ran along the entire East Coast.

For the whole ride, she thought she'd been duped. It seemed like this Outcast guy was just an ordinary citizen, working a regular nine-to-five. She had already planned on paying Dreads a visit down at the jail once she got back. The U.S. Attorney would accompany her this time as she marched down there and presented him with an indictment. However, things began to change once she saw Outcast pull up to this green and white middle class home.

"Bravo team, you copy?" she whispered into the radio. "Bravo team here, copy."

"Get the U.S. Attorney on the phone and have them contact a Magistrate asap. Let them know that we have a possible drug distribution enterprise going on, and that we-" she stopped at the sight of a .357 Smith and Wesson revolver. She didn't know what to expect as she stared at the man who held her life in the palm of his hands.

"Repeat that for me Alpha. You faded off towards the end, copy?"

She heard Bravo team cackle back over the radio but couldn't respond. They had no idea she was being held at gunpoint, stuck, staring at the tip of a barrel.

Agent Bradley took a deep breath as she prepared herself for what was going to happen next. In that moment, all she could think about was how she was about to see her brother.

***

Cash and Juan's team of killers arrived in Galveston, Texas, right outside Houston around 3 am. At least forty of Felix's men were waiting for them when they landed. They had guns, vests, and plenty of ammunition already put together. When they pulled out of the small private airport, Cash got back on the phone.

"Hello!" he said after hearing someone pick up.

"What's good my nigga?" asked Trap, unaware of what was taking place.

"I'm out here in Texas taking care of business as we speak. Ghost gave me the green light, so we had to move fast."

"What?" he shot back in disbelief. He was confused and didn't understand how he could just let him miss out on their plan to get revenge. The thought of putting Migo and his uncles in a grave is what made his hard work worthwhile.

"How you..." he paused, realizing he was talking too loud. He got up from the bed and walked into the living room, hoping Tameka would remain sleep. "How you gone move without me cuzz?" he asked bitterly.

Cash leaned his head back and massaged the bridge of his nose. He knew Trap wanted to get payback just as much as he did, but it wasn't up to him. If he wanted to eliminate the Zetas, and get them out the way, he had to do it on Felix's time, and not his.

"Homie, you know if it was up to me, you'd be right here beside me, but it ain't."

He knew he was right. Not in a million years would Cash betray him like that. They had been through too much not to believe him.

"Alright then fam," he replied, not wanting to discuss the matter any further over the phone, "just be careful, because if any-"

"It won't," Cash interjected, already knowing where the conversation was going. He knew Trap like the back of his hand. If anything were to happen to him, he would try and seek revenge on every cartel member known to mankind. He had already lost two of his best friends, so to lose another one would probably be the news to take him over the edge.

"Enough said then my nigga, one hunnid!"

"One."

Click!

Without say it, he informed him to wake everyone up. They were about to finish a job they'd been working on and needed to pull in all resources to keep their families safe. A code black was issued, which meant cease and dismiss all movement until further notice. No more chances would be taken, because all of their cards were on the table. This was the moment they'd been waiting for. The moment that lasted long enough for them to want it more than anything else in the world. Revenge. The feeling Tupac rapped about in his hit some *Hail Mary*.

He knew there was a possibility he could die during this mission, but he didn't care. He was a part of something major, and the circumstances required for him to get his hands dirty. He looked forward to seeing his old friends, and new enemies. They would have the luxury of meeting their maker very soon, the thought of it bringing him pleasure.

He assumed Jasmin and Shay had made it home already, so he called Jasmin's cell. He wanted to talk to his baby before went down. He knew hearing her voice would make him a little weak, but he knew it would also remind him what he had to get back home to.

CHAPTER 15

HOSPITALITY

"Thank you so much, Warren," she thanked the man, reaching out to grab the cup of coffee he prepared for her.

"Now don't be going off and thanking me just yet," he replied, dismissing her appreciation as if it was nothing. "I'm just doing what any member of a law enforcement agency would do. After all, you're one of the good guys." He gave her an inviting smile, passing her his deceased wife's favorite coffee mug.

She smiled, letting him know how much she appreciated his hospitality. It was the least he could do after scaring her half-to-death.

Luckily for her, when he found her snooping around his property, he decided to give her the benefit of the doubt before blowing her head off. He could tell from how focused she was surveilling the house across the street, his home wasn't in any danger.

So, after nearly killing her for snooping around his property, he invited her in for some coffee. He also figured it wouldn't hurt to allow her to continue surveilling the home. To him, it was an honor to have a federal agent stake out at his home.

Warren was a retired Fayetteville Police Officer. After serving 4 years in the Marines, he took a mediocre paying job on the force to keep him active. He patrolled the Ville's raged streets for twenty-five years before deciding it was enough. Him and his wife, Anna, had made plans to travel the world together once he retired, but after 5 long unsuccessful years of fighting Cancer, he was left alone to travel as far as his heart would take him. He missed her dearly but watching Agent Bradley take sips from her old coffee mug seemed to bring him some joy. In his mind, it was like she was carrying on her memory.

"So, how long have you stayed here, Warren?" she asked, placing the cup down so she could look back through her binoculars.

"Twenty-two years," he stated proudly, reflecting back on some of the most memorable moments he shared with Anna inside their home.

"Wow!" she stated, partly listening as she watched the Dodge Magnum back into the driveway across the street. It was the third car she'd seen in the past two hours do the same exact thing.

Back in. Load up. Then pull out.

Somebody was definitely moving something, and she couldn't wait for her intuition to prove her right.

"Come in Alpha team, this is Charlie, you copy?"

Passing the binoculars over to Warren, she snatched the radio from her belt clip and radioed back. "Alpha team here, copy." Warren, not knowing whether she wanted him to hold them or take a peek, decided to be a little nosy. He held them up to his face and took a look.

"Copy, did you see that?"

She rolled her eyes, thinking, 'Yeah you idiot, I'm standing

right across the street.'

"Copy that, Charlie, I saw it. When he pulls off, have FPD follow him as well, alright?" The other two cars that had come and gone were also being tailed.

"Copy Alpha, Charlie out."

"Bravo team, copy?" she said, switching communication.

"Copy, Bravo here, Alpha."

"What's the status on that warrant. I needed that shit like yesterday." She was growing impatient by the minute. More and more boxes were leaving the residence, and she feared if they took any longer, there wouldn't be any evidence left for them to confiscate.

"They're waking the judge up now, Alpha. They should have it signed in a matter of minutes."

That was music to her ears.

"Alright then, Bravo. Have the Marshal's Office on standby with an Engagement Team. We are gonna take these fuckers down, copy?"

"Copy that, Alpha team, Bravo out."

The sweet smell of victory was in the air. It was so close to her she could almost taste it.

Brrrrrt!

"Excuse me!" Warren apologized, farting for the second time. The first one he let go was silent, that's why she didn't catch it at first. After realizing the funk in the air was not the glory she'd been expecting, but the repugnant odor of the white man's ass standing beside her, she nearly threw up.

"I hope a little gas doesn't bother you," he continued nonchalantly, never looking away from the binoculars as if it wasn't a problem.

"Nah!" she replied disgusted, pulling her crew neck over her nose to muffle the stench he was killing her with. She shook her head. She couldn't help but appreciate the fact that he didn't kill her in the backyard.

***

"Take off your shirt so I can see what you're working with," Tiffany giggled, licking her lips from anticipation of seeing some muscles.

TP, Square, and Juvi were all in Mercedees dorm room playing Strip Monopoly, and Juvi had just rolled the dice landing on Tiffany's property. In return for payment, she instructed him to give her a piece of his property, meaning his personal property. You could tell by looking around the room, the girls were obviously winning. All the boys were bare chested with no socks, shoes, or belts. TP was down to his boxers, but he didn't care. The seductive look on Mercedees face let him know that she could see his dick print through the soft fabric.

The girls, on the other hand, was still fully clothed. At the beginning of the game, they had all agreed to buy as much property as they could. They knew from experience the key to winning the game because the played it often.

The boys were no match for them.

"Ugh uhm, ladies," Mercedees muttered, looking over at the 3 half-naked men before them, "looks like we got us some strong looking brothers up in this bitch tonight," she laughed, high fiving her two friends.

The guys didn't like being the only ones showing skin.

They only agreed to play because they assumed it wouldn't take too much for the girls to get naked. From the looks of it though, their assumption was wrong.

"Girl, you ain't lying," Vanessa chimed in, leaning over and licking TP's bicep.

"Ugh...ugh...ughmmm," Mercedees grunted, the expression on her face saying, 'no you didn't.'

Vanessa looked over at her friend and rolled her eyes. She forgot Mercedees had already claimed sexy ass TP, but after seeing his meat move around in his boxers, she couldn't help but get a sample.

"You bitches trippin'," Tiffany crowed, after watching her friends exchange dirty looks. She got up and walked over to the light, "this is what y'all need."

"What the fuck is you doing, Tiff?" Mercedees asked, not able to see anything after she cut the light off.

"Hold on, bitch!" she shot back jokingly.

Tiffany walked over to her dresser and grabbed a lighter. She went around the room lighting candle after candle until she could see everyone's faces. She was trying to set the mood so they could eventually get it on and popping. She wasn't trying to lay claim to anyone. Her plan was to get the party started.

"Now, isn't that better?" she said, pulling her shirt over her head and tossing it to the side.

The guys looked at one another and grinned. This was more like it. They knew the freak was bound to come out of any one of them, so they were glad when it finally did.

"Man, ya girl know how to run a show don't show," TP quipped, grabbing ahold of his boxers as his dick stood at nine o'clock.

Tiffany's c-cup breast demanded attention as she stood there waiting on her friends to follow suit.

Mercedees rolled her eyes and said, "TP, come over here."

It was more of an order than a request, but he didn't have a problem with her being in control. In fact, that's what he preferred. He stood up with his dick in his hand, and walked over to her, passing Tiffany along the way.

She looked him up and down, enjoying the full view of his muscular body as he passed, and decided to take claim to hi friend she'd been eyeing all night. "Come on, Square," she said, reaching down and grabbing his hand. She led him over to her bed and made him sit. The candlelight flickered off of her honey-colored skin as she slid her jeans down to her ankles. Stepping out of them, she took ahold of his hands and placed them on her thighs, waiting on him to take off the rest of her clothes.

After watching the two porno scenes begin, Juvi crawled over to Vanessa and stuck his tongue in her mouth. She hungrily accepted it, pulling him in closer so he could wrap his arm around her. They paused long enough to give him time to pull her shirt and pants off. The red Victoria's Secret panty and bra set she was wearing made her even more desirable. Her dark skin with hazel brown eyes looked good on her petit frame. Assuming her pussy tasted as good as she looked, without any hesitation, he pulled her panties off and dove headfirst between her legs.

TP and Mercedees were both laying naked on the bed as they tried making their way to home base. She was busy licking his nipples while her hands gently stroked his dick, her body over top of his. He gasped as her mouth made its way down to his genitalia. It was a feeling out of this world, and he wanted to return the favor, but she acted first, skillfully continuing to suck his dick, Karren Stephen's style. She maneuvered the bottom half of her body over his head so her moist pussy could stare him in the eyes. TP gripped her thighs and plunged forward, his tongue leading the charge as it parted her pink lips.

"Mhmmm" and "ahhhh" were the only noises being made in the room as everyone enjoyed the road to euphoria.

***

Boom!

Pop! Pop! Pop!

Pop! Pop! Pop!

It was on and popping. The grenade that blew the gate off its hinges, allowed Cash and his crew to enter in through the front of Migo's Estate. There was another team coming in from the backside of the mansion to ensure that no one escaped.

Cash jumped out of the black SUV carrying an assault rifle as the vehicle came to an abrupt halt near the front door. This was not the same house he had visited before on prior occasions where he picked the load up, however, because of his loyal contacts in Houston, he was able to keep up with his whereabouts. From the looks of it, Migo had stepped his game up. Compared to his old crib, this one exhibited a higher level of prominence that could only be equated to a bigger drug distribution network. They had obviously been getting richer while he was recovering from his gunshot wound.

"Cash!" he heard Juan bellow through the walkie talkie.

"Yeah!" he shouted back, taking cover behind the door frame near the entrance. Shots were coming from the living room, but they couldn't place the position of the shooter.

Pop! Pop! Pop!

Pop! Pop! Pop!

He returned fire as bullets chopped at the wood on the other side of the frame. The gun battle was intense. He could tell from hearing the rapid gun fire coming from the back of the house, the team coming in from the rear was having trouble penetrating the house as well.

"Cash!" he heard Juan call again.

He grabbed his walkie talkie, getting ready to snap on him for constantly shouting his name, when Juan radioed back, "their dead!"

He couldn't believe it. Manny and Negro was really dead. The news of hearing the two uncles fate brought a pleasant smile to his face.

Juan was instructed to take out the uncles while Cash attended to Migo. The assaults were taking place simultaneously, at two different locations. Juan had already completed his mission and would probably be on his way back to Mexico at any moment.

"Are you sure it's them, Juan?" he radioed back after sending a few shots through the front window. He signaled for the two Mexicans on the opposite side of the door to go in through the window as he held the position down in the front.

"Si, estoy seguro," Juan replied confidently, "what's the status on Migo?"

He didn't have any good news as of yet, but he was working on it. The two Mexicans he'd ordered to climb through the window had prevailed on their task and eliminated the gunman in the living room. He knew any minute now, he would have an opportunity to report the same victory back to his comrade.

"Hey, amigo, todo esta claro," he heard one of them shout from the living room, letting him know that everything was clear. Cash slowly entered the house, his rifle leading the way as he approached the living room. As he entered he noticed one of the Mexicans from his team was on a wall clutching his shoulder.

He'd been shot, but the wound didn't appear to be life threatening. Cash gave him the thumbs up, and he nodded in return, letting him know that he was good. Then, he walked over to the other one who was searching the victim he'd just killed.

Cash had never known Migo to keep so many armed bodyguards at his home, but obviously the war with Felix had intensified, so he must have anticipated this day coming.

"Cash!" Juan called over the radio again.

He had forgotten he was still waiting on a status check. Just when he was about to reply, gunfire erupted from the balcony overlooking the downstairs corridor. Him and the two Mexicans dove on the floor to avoid the hail of bullets.

They were relieved when they realized the gunfire was not intended for them. It was meant for the team that was coming in from the rear. The exchange of fire lasted about 15 seconds before it finally ceased.

Cash got back on his feet and walked over to one of them. "Have you found him?" he asked, referring to Migo.

"No, senor."

"Damn!" he complained, wondering how he could have slipped through his fingers. "Search this house completely before we leave, understand?"

Everyone nodded.

"Juan!" He radioed back.

"Si, que paso?"

"We haven't found him yet," he replied disappointed.

He knew that wasn't a good look because they needed to get Migo as well.

"Don't worry about it my friend. Move out and meet me back at jefe's, okay!"

He was listening, but his attention was on something that looked out of place. There was something off about the fireplace that caught his attention. He walked over to it, observing it for a minute before it hit him.

There was a crack, hardly noticeable to the eye, between the floorboard and, fireplace. With his fingers, he traced the seam, following it all the way around the perimeter. He didn't know what he was looking for, but he knew it was something important.

"Amigo, que paso?" one of the Mexicans inquired, stepping back into the room after completing his search.

Cash glanced up at him, then back down at the fireplace. He had an idea. "Step back and take cover," he ordered, walking up to him and snatching one of his grenades off his jacket. The Mexican looked at him like he was crazy after watching him pull the pin and toss it in the fireplace.

"Grenada!" he yelled running out of the room.

Ba-boom!

The house rattled and shook from the blast, spewing dust all over the living room. When they reentered and saw the results, they knew exactly where Migo disappeared too.

"Juan!" he called over the radio.

"I'm in pursuit of him now, but I'm probably gonna need some assistance."

"Alright, my friend, I'm boarding a chopper now," he replied, "Where are you?"

"I'm in a tun- in- Mi-," his radio was breaking up, and Juan couldn't understand what he was saying.

"Repeat that again," he shouted.

"I'm -n a -nel on -y way -"

Juan couldn't understand anything he was saying. All he knew was that they were in Houston, so he directed the pilot to stay in the area until he heard from him again. Felix wanted Migo and his uncles dead, and he knew whatever his boss wanted, that's what he got.

***

Beep! Beep!

Ring! Ring!

Chirp! Chirp!

T P, Square, and Juvi all heard their phones going off, letting them know they had messages. Amid their freak session, they all stopped and grabbed their phones.

"What the fuck is wrong with y'all?" Tiffany complained, not pleased with the sudden interruption.

Square was in the middle of eating her ass out when he hopped off the bed. Her ass was still in the air waiting on him to return when the light came on.

"Oh my god!" Mercedees exclaimed, disgusted by her friend's ass hole. "Put that black hole up before it sucks us all up," she joked, covering herself up as well.

Tiffany was so embarrassed. She snatched the blanket to cover her body and whined, "Square, why did you do that?"

Both of her friends were laughing at how nasty she was. They were getting their freak on as well, but the idea of getting their ass ate out from the back was not one of their minds.

After reading their messages, the guys started getting dressed.

"Aye, y'all get dressed," TP instructed the girls before walking over to Mercedees. "Babe, we gotta get you out of here."

"For what?" she scoffed. "What's going on?" she asked, following instructions as she put on her clothes.

From what seemed like out of nowhere, all 3 of the guys produced a firearm. The girls hadn't noticed earlier when they entered the room, they slid their handguns under Tiffany's bed.

"Oh my god!" Vanessa gasped at the sight of the weapons. "Why do y'all have those?"

They didn't have time to explain to her what was going down. All they knew was that they had to get Mercedees to a safe location and fast.

"Ma, we don't have time to go through this right now," Juvi informed her, checking his pistol to make sure he had a round already loaded into the chamber. "Either you are coming with us, or you're not, but we gotta get her outta here now," he finished with his finger pointed over at Mercedees.

"Girl, just come on," Mercedees told her, frustrated. She already knew what was going on. Something happened again, and her brother was involved. She understood they had a job to do, but that's what bothered her the most. Last time she lost a brother, so she secretly feared that this time she would lose another.

CHAPTER 16

BIG MISTAKE

"Are you trying to tell me that you are selling cosmetic products out of the back of your house?" Agent Bradley asked skeptically. "That's exactly what I am trying to tell you," Jay assured her. He wasn't sure whether she was buying his story or not, but it was the only story he had to offer her. Agent Bradley was not expecting her case to turn for the worse. After receiving word that a Magistrate signed off on the warrant, her teams of agents, aided by the U.S. Marshall's office, commenced on Jay's residence. To her surprise, there were no drugs on the premises. Only boxes of soap and deodorant.

"Don't fucking lie to me you piece of shit!" she growled, upset more with herself than with him. The dogs hadn't picked up any scent of drugs yet, and she was becoming more frustrated by the minute.

Jay was frightened by her sudden outburst. He knew she was upset because she had thought they made a major bust.

"Agent Bradley!" she heard one of her co—workers call her. When she looked over towards the agent, she saw him signal for her to come and get the phone. She knew whoever was on the other end would probably not have any good praises for her hard work. She had messed up big time, and in the midst, caused the agency resources, time, and money.

As she walked over and grabbed the phone, rolling her eyes at the agent, she answered, "This is Agent Bradley."

For what seemed like an hour, but was only 3 minutes, she listened to her boss chew her up and spit her out. He was not pleased and complained about her negligence. She thought about interrupting his moment of bashing to remind him of all the hard work shed done for the Bureau, but decided against it. Her obsession in catching Trap led her down a destructive path, and she secretly regretted her decision to pursue him. For the next 6 months, she imagined how boring desk work would be.

"Yes, sir," she replied on the brink of tears. She was exhausted, and to hear her boss really go in on her like this hurt her feelings. The Bureau was all she had, but to know she'd caused them so much really weighed in on her.

Her boss instructed for her to clean up her mess and be in his office first thing in the morning. She would be formally reprimanded for her latest failure, and more than likely be reassigned to a desk job. Her career in the field was over, and she knew it.

"Agent Bradley," another agent rushed over towards her with a phone to his ear, "we got a break!"

Her eyes went wide with excitement, "What is it?" she asked, forgetting all about her boss on the line.

"One of the cars that was stopped," he paused to make sure she was paying attention.

She nodded, urging him to continue.

"The driver confessed, giving up details about where the dope is hidden."

It was music to her ears.

Here she was thinking her life was almost down the drain, when her brother reached down from the heavens and blessed her. Remembering she had her boss on the line, she put the phone to her ear and said, "Let me get back to you, I'm onto something."

Then she hung up.

She listened as the agent continued to break down the details. She looked over at Jay who was not looking so innocent after all. He had been lying the whole time, and she couldn't wait for the opportunity to make him pay for it. If it wasn't for one of the carriers cracking under pressure, they would've had no choice but to cut him loose. But, after hearing everything he had, she walked back over and smiled. He was about to be her latest victim and didn't even know it.

***

Running nonstop, he didn't think it would ever end. When his eyes finally saw an opening at the end of the tunnel, he breathed a sigh of relief. The tunnel, which was Migo's escape route, ran into another home about a mile and half away from his residence. Cash and the two Mexicans from his team, ran through it in hopes of catching up with him, but by the time they made it through, he was already gone.

"Damn!" Cash stressed to himself, realizing Migo had gotten away.

The house they were in was completely empty. The only evidence that Migo had been there, was the trail of dirty footprints that traveled from the tunnel to the front door.

Exiting the home he noticed the sun was rising. Checking his watch he realized it was six-fifteen. He knew the police would find the tunnel and be there soon, so he did the first thing to come to his mind.

He figured, for Migo to escape, there must have been a car sitting in the front to aid him in his escape. People in the neighborhood surely notice it, so without advising his companions about his new plan, he walked next door and kicked the door in. The Mexicans didn't know what he was doing, but they followed him anyways. He instructed them to search the house, but not to kill anyone if they could help it. He was winging it the best way he knew how, and didn't need an unnecessary body count to complicate the situation.

As he began searching upstairs, he came across a young Hispanic couple who were still in their bed. Noticing the man was about to get up, Cash warned him between clenched teeth to remain still.

"Don't fuckin' move!"

"What the hell is going on?" the guy asked, raising his hands up so Cash can see them.

"Listen," Cash lowered his gun in order to keep them calm. "All I need from you folks is a little information, alright?"

Awaken by the strange voice in her bedroom, the woman cowered near her significant other. At the same time, the two Mexicans with Cash entered the room.

"Dinero, esta claro," one of them informed him, letting him know the rest of the house was all clear.

"Okay, wait downstairs, I'm on my way."

The two Mexicans glanced at the scared couple and nodded. They were pressed for time, so they followed his instructions with no hesitation.

"Look!" Cash stated, making sure he had their attention.

"Describe the car that's usually parked outside the house next door?"

The couple looked at each other confused.

"Come on, come on, I'm running out of time here," he urged them.

"What are you talking about?" the woman asked.

"The car, the car," he repeated, assuming they knew what he was talking about.

"There's never a car parked next door," the man replied shaking his head, "only a motorcycle."

Bingo!

That was all he needed to know. He started off towards the door before another idea crossed his mind. Turning around, he asked, "Where's your car keys?"

The man hesitated for a minute before telling him they were downstairs hanging on the hook by the refrigerator. He wanted this intruder out of his home as soon as possible, even if it meant giving him his car.

Cash rushed downstairs, grabbed the keys, and ran out the front door. He knew they would call the police the minute he pulled off, so he instructed the Mexicans to go back upstairs and tie them up before they left.

"Juan, where are you?" he called over his radio.

"It's about time you hit me back," Juan replied, "Where are you?"

"Migo escaped through a tunnel about a mile away from his home, so that's why we lost contact. But listen," he crunk up the couple's Kia Sonata, and pulled out to the curb, are you still airborne?"

"Si, but we only got enough fuel for about thirty more minutes."

"Good, that's plenty of time. Be on the lookout for a red motorcycle leaving this area. If you spot it, let me know where, because that's him, alright?"

"Alright, I'll let you know if we come across it."

Cash watched the two Mexicans emerge from the home as he shouted for them to come on. He radioed Juan and told him where to start his search.

Ten minutes hadn't even passed before he radioed back, "He's on the interstate headed south."

***

"I can't believe this shit, Trap! Where the fuck is he?" Jasmin asked angrily. She was fed up with not knowing what was going on. She didn't spend months nursing Cash back to health just so he could go back out there and get himself killed.

"J, why are you giving me the third degree? Didn't he call you this morning and let you know what was going on?" Trap asked in his defense. He knew exactly where Cash was, but refused to tell her, because he knew she would go off. They paused at the sound of the front door closing.

Mercedees, followed by five more people came walking into the living room where they were.

"Jasmin, is my brother here?" She asked worriedly without acknowledging Trap.

"No," she replied with an attitude, "and this nigga won't tell me where the fuck he is!" She rolled her eyes at Trap as she walked out of the room and into the kitchen.

"Big homie, we got here as soon as we could. What's poppin?" TP asked, walking over and giving him dap.

"Who are they?" Trap asked, pointing at Tiffany and Vanessa. TP looked over at the girls and then back at Trap.

"They were with her when we retrieved her, so we brought them along as well."

Trap shook his head, displeased with their failure to follow instructions. He gestured for TP, Juvi, and Square to follow him outside so they could discuss what was going on.

He didn't need everyone, especially any outsiders knowing what was happening, so he told them to stay in the house as he discussed matters with the guys.

"Girl, I thought you said your brothers were dead?" Tiffany probed, walking over and sitting next to Mercedees. Vanessa decided to sit on the opposite side of her.

"Please don't start asking me questions right now, okay!" She told them. She was too busy trying to figure things out to be answering any questions.

Jasmin walked back into the living room with a glass of water and looked at them. They were guests in her home, but she wasn't in the mood to be showing anyone any kind of hospitality. Trap disturbed her peace, and she didn't know if she could continue living her life like this. She needed Cash to be there for her and their baby. He owed her that much, and she'd be damned if she didn't have it that way.

***

Once they were outside away from the girls, Trap filled them in on what was going down. He informed them that Cash was in Texas taking care of their unfinished business, but needed for everyone to be on alert just in case things didn't turn out how he expected. He wasn't sure whether the outcome would be a good, but he assured them that the Zetas would be a distant memory after today.

"Hello," he answered his cell on the second ring. "What's crackin', my nigga?"

"Not too much right now family, but what's good? Kind of early for to be callin' me, ain't it?"

"Yeah, it is, but I'm about to be ghost for the next week and I need to pay my rent."

Trap knew that was code for debt.

"Well, call Olivia and have her meet you somewhere then," he told the caller, not wanting to leave Cash's crib until he heard from him.

"Man, I already thought about that dawg, but she didn't answer the phone. Plus, I don't really like her all in our business, fam. If you're not gonna pick it up now, then I'll have it for you when I get back."

Trap didn't like the sound of having to wait a whole week for his money, but what else could he do.

"Alright but check it out. Make sure you hit me back the minute you return, okay?"

"Yeah, I got you dawg, one!"

"One!" Trap hung up and continued his conversation.

***

"Do we got a lock on that location," Agent Bradley shouted to the technician tracing the call.

"Yes, we do. It's near a residence in Richmond Hill, Georgia."

"Beautiful, fucking beautiful," she clapped her hands together in celebration. "You did good kid, you did real good," she congratulated Jay.

Once she brought it to his attention that she knew the dope was hid in the cosmetics, he started talking. He told them about Trap, Olivia, and the other hubs along the coast that made up their whole distribution network. The thought of him going back to prison for an indefinite amount of time was enough to get him to cooperate. Luckily, in exchange for his full cooperation, he would be granted immunity from any prosecution. It was a deal of a lifetime considering the fact they were able to retrieve all the dope he'd distributed to his couriers.

"That's all y'all need from me, right?" he stated, hoping his job was done.

"Not so fast kiddo," said one of the agents. "Until we arrest everyone involved, you're going to stay in our custody. Officer, please escort him down to the jail for us."

Jay shook his head in disbelief. He thought once he set-up Trap, he would be free to leave, but the Fed's wasn't having it.

Once he was in the car, and on his way down to Fayetteville County Jail, Agent Bradley got on the phone.

"Boss, I'm going to need the Marshals assistance in 3 states." She picked up a piece of paper and started reading off the cities," Palm Beach, Florida, Savannah, Georgia, and New York, New York."

***

"Este loco de negro," he heard one of the Mexicans say as he weaved back and forth through traffic. Cash was dedicated to completing his mission, and if that made him crazy, he planned on being the craziest man alive.

They were on the interstate where Juan said he saw the red motorcycle heading south. Doing well beyond the speed limit, he didn't give a damn about the police. If they had the nerve to interfere in his pursuance of Migo, then he would have no other choice but to shoot it out with them as well. That's just how serious the situation had gotten. If Migo found out he was still alive, he would not be able to get a good night's rest. This beef between him and his old friend had to end today, no matter what.

"Juan, where are you?" he spoke into the walkie talkie. There was some static coming through before he heard him clearly.

"We're loading up right now, Dinero. What do you want me to do?"

"I need you to cut him off," Cash replied, unaware if Migo had gotten off at one of the exits they'd already passed.

"I don't know where he's going, but if he's still on the highway, I want y'all to cut him off, got it?"

"Si, I got you."

Cash sped up a little. His intuition was kicking him in the back of the head urging him to keep on going. He had no clue as to where Migo could be headed, but if he caught up with him, he was going to make sure it was the last time they ever saw each other alive.

"We're on the highway heading your way now," Juan informed him.

Using tunnel vision, Cash peered ahead through the scarce traffic to locate his target. He knew Juan couldn't be too far away, so if they happened to meet each other without seeing Migo, that meant he'd gotten away. The clock was running out of time and so was the space between him and Juan. He beat on the steering wheel out of frustration of possibly losing the only opportunity he had of getting his man. Then, just when he didn't think things could get any worst, the gas light came on, warning him he only had 8 miles of gas left.

"Shit," he panted, not knowing what else to do. Not only was he running out of time and fuel, he was running out of options. The forces of the universe were not on his side, and he knew it. Just when he was about to let up off the accelerator, he heard the Mexican next to him say, "Mida!"

Looking towards where the Mexican's short finger was pointed, Cash saw the red motorcycle. He grabbed the walkie talkie from his shoulder, but before he could press the button to speak, Juan said, "I see it, Dinero! I see it! The red motorcycle is about to pass us now."

***

"Whatever you do, don't let anyone leave the residence, is that clear?" Agent Bradley whispered through her radio to the teams on standby.

"Bravo team here, that's a copy."

"Charlie team copy as well."

Agent Bradley, now backed by Delta Team, was about to pull onto Cash's residence. Bravo Team was staked out in the woods surrounding the home, while Charlie Team took position at all exit routes. The whole area was secured and blocked off. No one could get in or get out.

From what Bravo Team informed her, there were numerous vehicles parked outside the home. Some of the tags read Chatham County, while a few others said Bibb. To her, it didn't matter where they were from as long as by the end of the day they were all in handcuffs. She signaled for the driver of the bullet proof suburban to pull up to the front. Everything was going to go pretty fast, but she was praying that no fatalities took place.

"Go, go, go!" she shouted over the radio.

Out of what seemed like nowhere, police vehicles, unmarked cars and agents all commenced on the home. Doors were being kicked in, while orders were being shouted for everyone to get on the ground. Police lights were flickering all over, as agent after agent entered the residence.

Agent Bradley, flanked by countless law enforcement personnel, was one of the first agents through the door. She moved throughout the home as if she knew it like the back of her hand, managing to get everyone on the ground without incident.

In the living room, Mercedees, her friends, Trap, and his soldiers were all sprawled out on the floor with zip ties secured around their wrists. Mercedees was cussing out everyone. She was a full-time college student attending Spelman, and thought they would have some compassion for her. To them, she was a potential suspect in their eyes and that's all that mattered.

Trap stayed calm, urging everyone else to do the same. In his mind, this was all just a big mistake and would be taken care of shortly once he had the opportunity to contact his attorney.

"What the fuck is going on?" Jasmin barked at the agents who were escorting her and Miss. Tina down the steps.

"Y'all better have a got damn warrant, I know that much!" she warned, cradling Legacy in her arms as she mugged the agents.

Trap raised his head off the floor and said, "Jaz, just do what they ask you and I promise everything will be okay."

"Don't be tryin' to keep me calm, Trap!" she shot back, snatching her arm away from the agent trying to restrain her.

Agent Bradley was on the phone speaking with the Marshall's Office in New York when she heard Jasmin refer to the guy on the ground as Trap. Although she would eventually know who everyone was, it caught her attention when she heard the name of the person she'd been wanting to see since day one.

"That's great news!" she spoke with excitement into the receiver. So far, the hub in New York and Florida had been taken down.

The Marshall's Office in Florida informed her that a shootout had occurred, but everything was now under control. Boxes of cosmetics were being confiscated from all over, and more and more suspects were being apprehended. The U.S. Attorney's Office was putting together an indictment for everyone involved. It was beginning to look like they had taken down one of the biggest drug operations this side of the country had ever seen, and it was all because of one agent's obsession with a drug dealer.

"Stand him up for me," she told one of the marshal's watching over the suspects in the living room.

When he pulled Trap to his feet, she walked up to him and smiled.

"This is all just a big mistake, and I'm sure, in a minute we are all going to be laughing about this," he told her, convinced that they had nothing.

She chuckled.

"I'm sure your right Mr.-" she paused to look at his ID, "Travis Porter, or would you prefer to be called Trap?"

He looked at her questionably, trying to figure her out. Did she know more than he gave her credit for? 'She can't have anything on me,' he thought to himself. He knew it would not be in his best interest to say anything without his lawyer, so he remained quiet.

She instructed the marshal to take him to her vehicle, but have the rest of them placed in the van. They would all be taken down to the county jail and processed until their arraignment hearing, but first, she wanted to see if he was willing to give up his connect.

***

Scurrrt…Boom!

Migo didn't even see it coming. The black Tahoe had come from the left side of the road and clipped his bike. The impact pushed him off the road and into the grass. He loss all control of the bike, hopping off it to avoid colliding with a tree. The motorcycle hit it straight on, causing an explosion. The tumbling of his body left his mind in disarray. Before he even got a chance to recollect himself, and get back on his feet, someone hit him in the face with a pistol, knocking him out cold. His body was then picked up and carried over to the SUV. He was tossed into the back seat where two men gagged and tied him up. By the time Cash pulled up, Juan's men were already carrying Migo to one of the trucks. He walked over to the vehicle they placed him in and aimed his pistol; that's when Juan stopped him.

"Dinero, we're taking him with us," he waved for Cash to get in the truck with him as the truck with Migo pulled off.

After instructing one of the Mexicans with him to get rid of the car, Cash and the other one ran over and got into the truck with Juan. They heard sirens approaching, so Juan told the driver to haul ass and blend in with the traffic up ahead.

"Why the fuck are we taking him with us?" Cash asked angrily. "We could have just put a bullet in his head and been out!"

"Remain calm my friend," Juan told him. "Jefe has instructed me to bring him back alive if possible."

Cash did not like the idea of Migo enjoying another minute of breath while his brother laid dead in the ground. The only thing separated him from a piece of mind and a world of chaos was Migo, and he didn't like it one bit.

He sat back and gathered his thoughts as he watched police car after police car pass them on the highway. The driver did a great job blending in with the early morning traffic, but he knew it would only get them so far. They had to get off the interstate and go somewhere safe.

"Juan, we gotta get off one of these exits if we're trying not to go to jail."

Juan looked at him and smiled.

"Don't worry my friend," he said casually, "in 2 hours we'll be in Mexico, and out of U.S. jurisdiction."

Cash looked ahead and saw the sign that supported his statement. They were approximately 152 miles away from the Mexico border. He didn't know how they planned on crossing it with Migo tied up in the other truck, but obviously he knew something Cash didn't. So, instead of complaining about what was going to happen, he remained silent. They would be in

Mexico soon, and hopefully from there, he would be back in GA with Jasmin and their child.

CHAPTER 17

TUPAC

"You have a collect call from, 'Travis'," Tameka heard the recording say after answering the phone. She had been waiting on this call all day. It was all over the news how one of the biggest drug operations to ever hit Georgia had been taken down. It was the BMF story all over again.

She pressed five to accept the call, then waited to hear the voice she desperately needed to hear.

She was an emotional wreck. The past 24-hours had been a nightmare. To see her cousin/lover's face plastered all over the news with so many others, let her know that her worst fear had come into realization. Trap was more than likely going to prison, just like her baby's father. She watched in awe as a federal prosecutor proclaimed to be in the process of constructing a 16-person indictment containing multiple charges of Conspiracy, Continuing Criminal Enterprise (CCE), and Racketeering Involving a Criminal Organization (RICO), along with a queue of other charges. Then on top of that, they had a hundred thousand dollar reward out for any information leading up to the arrest of Cashmere Lewis.

That caught her by surprise. Investigators said that they recovered fingerprints and traces of DNA belonging to him at a home in Richmond Hill after a raid had taken place. He was immediately placed on America's Most Wanted top 10 fugitive list. A story was displayed on CNN about him and his brother, Money, who were allegedly killed almost a year ago. The news media was eating the story up. The indictment was getting longer and longer, adding more and more suspects by the hour. They were even talking about a Senator's daughter being involved in the organization.

Tameka didn't know what to think, but she knew whatever Trap needed her to do, she would do it.

"Hello," he said, once the call came through.

"Oh my God, baby, what did you do?" she cried, not able to hold back her emotions.

He expected her to respond this way. He knew when he dialed her number she would be upset, but he had no one else to call. He couldn't get in contact with Cash because he knew the Fed's would be monitoring him 24/7. Tameka knew enough to take care of the things he needed her to take care of, so he made it his business to call her first.

"I know everything seems cloudy right now boo, but stay with me. I need you to be strong for me Meek and not let this shit get you upset." He heard her crying reduce to a sniffle, so he knew she was trying to regain her composure.

"Okay," she agreed, sounding like a kid attempting to follow instructions. She gathered herself, placing her emotions in check.

"What do you need me to do, Travis?"

"Listen," he said, "first, I need you to contact my lawyer for me, and tell him to bond out everyone who gets a bond. I really don't think they're gonna give me a bond right now Meeka, but make sure Jasmin and all of them get out."

"Why won't they give you a bond?" she inquired sadly.

"Because that's how these people operate. They got me as one of the heads in this conspiracy, so I know they are gonna be reluctant in letting me go." He knew it was not likely he would be getting out anytime soon. Some of the things Agent Bradley threw his way during her attempt to interrogate him let him know that things were not looking good.

Olivia had been arrested, and all of her businesses had been federally seized. Reporters were beating her father's door down seeking comments about his daughter's alleged ties to the illegal drug trade. He was embarrassed by all the negative publicity. It was an election year, and the rumor that he could somehow be involved was not going to be good for his campaign.

Trap knew somebody was talking but didn't have a clue as to who. He had taken care of Bags himself, so whoever was snitching, had to be directly involved in their inner circle. Agent Bradley wouldn't offer him that little piece of information, probably because of how her last snitch turned out.

"Don't worry about me right now though, cause I'm good. Make sure you get in contact with my lawyer and have him do that. I talked to him for a brief moment already, but he's waiting on you to call before he proceeds.

The main reason he needed her to contact his attorney was to give him the money to take care of the bonds for everyone. He didn't feel safe talking about it over the phone because if the Feds knew how much money she was holding for him, she'd be getting picked up next.

"Did you know they got an award out for Cash?" she asked, unaware he already knew.

"Yeah, they think my nigga still alive," he replied, cleverly. "I feel sorry for Ms. Tina and all of them for having to relive their death all over again."

"So, he's really-"

"Meeka," he cut her off, "please just let that go, okay." He wasn't going to be discussing anything about Cash over the phone. The fact that he was alive was still up for discussion. The Feds were only going off the traces of DNA they found at the house. Nobody could concretely say he was alive except family and his most trusted men, and he hoped it stayed that way.

"Alright Trap," she replied, feeling bad for probing, "I'm just confused that's all. I miss you, and I don't want to lose you." Trap shook his head. He had gotten involved with his cousin sexually, and that was bad. To hear her say how much she missed him hurt him to his heart. She had been begging him to leave the game alone, but the chance of them getting to spend the rest of their lives together was questionable. The charges he was facing was serious, calling for him to do some real time. He wouldn't allow her to place her life on hold for him. That wasn't love. Although she completed him in so many ways, filling the void in his life he never knew existed, he was eventually going to have to let her go.

"You won't lose me, Meeka, I promise. But this may not play out how you may-"

"Don't talk like that," she interjected, cutting his pessimistic perspective short. "Everything is gonna be fine Travis. Just stay strong and have faith." It was her turn to give him some words of encouragement. Even though his future wasn't looking good, she still wanted him to be strong. Strong for himself, and strong for their baby."

***

"Great job Cash," Felix smiled, patting him on the back as he passed him a drink.

They were back in Mexico, out of the U.S. Government's jurisdiction. Cash assumed they were going to be crossing the border by way of the checkpoint when Felix surprised him again with an underground tunnel. The tunnel started at a warehouse about a mile and a half away from the border. When they first pulled into the warehouse, he thought they were just going to be swapping out vehicles, but after a forklift removed a pallet full of tortilla shells away from a spot on the floor, he knew what time it was. He had had heard of the infamous drug lord El Chapo using underground tunnels to smuggle drugs into the U.S. but had not actually seen one for himself. The construction of it was remarkable. A rail car line ran all the way through it, with tiny little lights along the way to give traffickers a way to see through the tunnel. It was drug smuggling in its finest form, and Cash was impressed.

"It wasn't all my doing Felix," he admitted, accepting the glass of Tequila and taking a swig. "Juan was the one to actually caught him."

"Nevertheless," he said, "it was with your help that we caught this punto, si?" He raised his glass up to congratulate him. "Well, to be quite honest Felix," Cash followed him as he left the kitchen, "it was not a part of the plan to bring him back alive. I don't need for this to come back and haunt me later on down the road. My plan was to kill everyone to ensure the safety of my family, and right now," he paused, waiting for Felix to stop walking and turn around.

"I don't feel like I've accomplished my mission."

Felix nodded his head as if he understood him clearly. He turned back around after hearing his gripe and took two steps forward, where he was now facing a door. He pulled a golden colored key from his pocket and opened it.

He looked back over to Cash and said, "Come downstairs with me for a minute my friend, and we'll continue the conversation down there. There's something I want to show you. He headed down the stairs as if he knew Cash would be right behind him.

Cash was upset and was beginning to feel like Felix was ignoring him. He was not comfortable with Migo still being alive. His life was at stake, and so was his family's. The remembrance of Migo's revenge against his frenemies played over and over again in his head and he didn't want his life to be the sequel to that display. He participated in killing his uncles, and that would not be forgiven.

However, since they did have him in their possession, he did feel like the ball was still in their court. So, he followed Felix down the narrow steps to see what kind of trick he had under his sleeve this time. Stepping off the last step, he looked around.

"Felix, you are a real piece of work," he said, walking over to where he was standing.

Felix chuckled at his statement.

"You see, my friend," he began, walking over and slapping Migo awake.

Smack!

Migo's eyes shot open. His naked body started wiggling erratically when he saw the faces of his captors. The chains that had him secured while he hung from the ceiling in the basement started rattling. He tried screaming and yelling for help, but the duct tape wrapped around his mouth only muffled his sounds.

"I got everything under control," Felix laughed maniacally, watching Migo's facial expression turn from anger to fear. The basement was totally black with only a single red-light bulb illuminating from the ceiling, right above Migo's face. Sitting right next to Migo was a toolbox with various little instruments that were obviously used for torture.

Cash smiled as he looked into Migo's hopeless eyes. He was looking like he'd seen a ghost or something. Seeing Cash alive only meant one thing for him. He was going to die.

Tink! Tink! Tink!

Felix tapped a cigar cutter on the toolbox to get his attention. He wanted him to see what he had in store for him.

"You see, Cash," he began, pulling a foot stool up to Migo so he could sit down where his feet were dangling, "the Zetas have been torturing my loved ones for information for a while now, so I plan on returning the favor."

Migo's eyes darted back and forth, from Cash to Felix as he panicked.

Felix grabbed ahold of his left foot and slid the cigar cutter over Migo's pinky toe. He looked up at him to see the look in his eyes as he chopped his toe off. Migo went crazy. He knew this was only the beginning of a long torture session.

To prevent him from bleeding out, Felix grabbed a bottle of alcohol mixed with petroleum jelly from off the toolbox and dapped a little bit of it on a cloth. He then took the cloth and covered the wound. The pain was unbearable, nearly making him pass out. The sound of hearing him squeal like a pig sent chills up Cash's spine.

Felix got up from the stool, pleased by his work, and walked over to Cash.

"It's your turn my friend, and please, think about your brother and how he died."

That was all he needed to get in the right mind frame. He walked over to Migo who was barely still conscious, and said, "Remember me, hermano?"

***

"All rise!" the bailiff announced loudly. "Now, presiding in this court of law, the honorable Judge Mathis."

"Damn, why this couldn't be the black nigga I use to see on TV?" Trap said to himself. He didn't like the look on the Magistrate's face. The pecker wood held a scowl, Trap interpreted as his I came to lynch a negro look.

The courtroom was jammed packed with family members, friends, and associates. The news media was not allowed inside the courtroom during their arraignment hearing, but Trap knew that would not stop them from receiving the story they planned on exploiting. Watching the latest headlines let him know that their drug operation was the next best thing to the singer Prince's death. The media was blowing it all out of proportion, causing them a whole bunch of unwanted publicity.

He looked over at Olivia and shook his head. Her and Jasmin was seated in the last row, while him and members of his crew sat in the first two.

Mercedees and her friends, along with Miss. Tina was subsequently released after the raid. The Fed's had no kind of evidence to link them to any of the charges. However, Jasmin remained in custody for aiding and abetting. Trap knew the charges against them had some merit, but he halfway still expected his attorney to get most of them dropped.

As they sat there in the courtroom, everyone held a worrisome look on their face; Everyone except Trap. He couldn't afford to wear his emotions on his sleeve. It would show a weakness in their unity, and he needed for everyone in the courtroom to know that him and his organization was strong.

"Seems like you have a lot on your hands with this case Ms. Johnson," the Judge said to the prosecutor.

"There's never a case too big for the U.S. Government, Judge Mathis. You know that," she replied with a smile.

Trap looked over at her table and saw the black female agent who was over their case. The fact that they were using two sisters to prosecute them made him sick. There was too much black-on-black violence tearing up the streets as it is to have to deal with it in the courtroom as well. He planned on using all the resources he had to let them know they weren't just messing with a random drug dealer. They would soon realize that they were messing with a real gangster.

"Ugh ummmm," his attorney cleared his throat. "I believe we have a hearing to proceed with."

Judge Mathis didn't like how the high-priced fancy attorney from Atlanta was trying to run his courtroom, but he knew he was right. The case before him was a high priority case, which called for him to conduct himself in a professional manner.

"As you wish, Mr. Lumpkin," he said, shuffling some papers around on his desk. "What says the Government?"

"Your honor, the charges brought by the Grand Jury are as follows..."

While she stated the 127 criminal charges, Trap wondered if Cash was okay. The last time he'd heard from him, he was on his way to take out Migo and his uncles, but that was three days ago. Somewhere in the news he remembered them talking about numerous shootings taking place in Texas, and it had Cash's name written all over it. The mission he was on called for that kind of publicity. The fact that his face was never revealed as being linked to any of them let him know that he'd gotten away. Either that, or Manny had gotten ahold of him for real this time. It bothered him to not know what was going on, but he had other things to worry about.

"Is that all?" The Judge asked, not surprised by the length of the indictment.

"That is it, your honor," she replied, sitting down next to Agent Bradley.

"Alright, then." Judge Mathis picked some papers up off his desk, glancing over them before he continued. "Are there any suggestions for bonds?"

"Ummm, to be honest Judge," she stood back up, "I believe all the male defendants should remain in custody of the Marshal's service until trial. These are serious charges, and the discovery is still in its developmental stage. Allowing any one of them to be released could be detrimental to our case."

"Your honor," Trap's attorney spoke up, "most of these defendants are without a criminal history, and it would be ridiculous for you not to grant any one of them a bond. My client-"

"Your client is the alleged leader in this conspiracy, am I right?" The Judge cut him off.

Mr. Lumpkin didn't quite know what to say. The indictment clearly identified Travis Scott as the leader of the CCE, RICO and Conspiracy, however, until twelve jurors decided he was in fact the leader, he would not accept allegations written on a piece of paper.

"Your honor, allegations are just that, allegations. We will have our day in court to determine guilt or innocence. For right now, procedurally it makes sense to grant some of the defendants a bond."

"Your honor, I will not oppose a bond for the women in this case, because I feel like their roles are minuscule," Ms. Johnson added.

"That doesn't seem to be the case with Ms. Mendez," replied Judge Mathis, referring to Olivia. "From what I am looking at Ms. Johnson, she was just as much involved as Mr. Porter, am I right?"

Olivia burst out crying loud enough for her father, who was seated in the pew, to hear. It was a cry for help. She halfway expected for him to jump up and demand that the judge set her free. That was the result she had in mind, but when the U.S. Marshal tapped her on the shoulder and told her to keep her emotions in check, she knew she was all alone. The look on her father's face let her know that it was out of his hands.

"Your honor, they have no record at all. I see no use in holding them, but the decision is yours.

Trap's attorney came over and whispered in his ear that it was a good chance he would not be getting a bond, but to remain strong. This was no surprise to him being that he'd been witnessing the dispute play out in front of him.

"Just get the girls outta here and a few of my niggas, and then we'll go from there, alright!" he whispered back.

Mr. Lumpkin nodded, then went back to addressing the court.

When it was all said and done, Trap and a few members from his crew remained in custody. The girls were released, as well as Twan, JJ, and Outcast. Smoke, who was in a wheelchair, was denied a bond almost immediately. The shootout he had in Palm Beach costed a Marshal three fingers, and the judge planned on showing him no mercy, Jay and TP was granted a bond while Square and Juvi was not. They both had records longer than Jay's, so that's why they weren't released. It was not the outcome Trap wanted, but at least somebody was getting out. He didn't know who the rat was in his crew, but he knew he had a better chance of getting to them on the outside than in witness protection.

When he heard the judge deny him bail, he smiled. It was the beginning to the end. The cards were all in and he was playing with a rigged deck. He was ready for war. The Fed's had made the first strike, destroying his peace. No one would no longer be safe, because the gloves were off. Federal Agent, Senator, or Judge. At this point, it didn't even matter. People lives were at stake. Dark clouds hovered above the courtroom as a sign that heavy storms were to come. When it rains, it pours, and when it pours, mother nature didn't care who it drowned.

Court was adjourned.

***

"Ahhhhhhh!" Migo screamed from behind the duct tape. The pain was driving him insane. For what seemed like a decade, he cried and wept begging for death. His eyelids had been snipped off by nail clippers, preventing him from closing his eyes, so he had no choice but to see it coming.

Cash and Felix took turns on him. While Cash was yanking his finger nails off with pliers, Felix was upstairs getting some rest. The torture chamber was soundproof, so Migo's cries for help would not be heard. When Felix returned though, to peel the skin off of Migo's dick, Cash went and enjoyed him a movie. They enjoyed taking their time with him. It was pure premeditated murder. Cash couldn't believe he was capable of such a thing, but when you're constantly put in a life and death situation, you eventually go numb to the value of life. He had been wronged by Migo and that's all that mattered. Thinking of Tupac's verse in Hail Mary brought a smile to his face, 'Revenge was the sweetest thing next to getting pussy'. Now that he had the chance to experience it for himself revenge had become his new high. It was a desire he never knew you could crave for. He had a passion and a new form of relief to give him pleasure. Whoever thought hearing a man cry sounded so damn good.

As he made his way back downstairs to participate in the brutal murder of his enemy, he heard his phone go off.

"Hello," he answered, wondering who was calling him from a restricted number.

"Read the text you just got," the caller said before hanging up.

Cash looked at his phone. After reading the coded message sent by numbers instead of words, he braced himself against the wall at the bottom of the steps. The caller had just let him know the Fed's had hit his home. Just when things were beginning to look good, everything went bad.

"What's wrong, Cash?" asked Felix, approaching him with bloody scissors in his hand.

"It's all bad, Felix," he stated with heavy concern written on his face.

Felix didn't understand. He was in the middle of cutting Migo's tongue out, because he was tired of hearing him scream. "The Fed's just hit us, Felix," he told him disappointingly.

It was not the kind of news you told your supplier, but he had to be upfront with him.

Felix didn't like losing money, but he wasn't going to allow that to stop him from working on Migo. "Let's not worry about that right now," he smiled, waving the scissors around in front of him. "We still got this punto over here to take our frustration out on. Plus, we'll figure something out. Don't worry about it."

Cash couldn't believe this maniac. Their whole operation was up in smoke, and he wanted to continue torturing Migo. That was not going to do it for him. He needed to get back to the States, and fast.

He looked past Felix and shook his head. "I'm gonna let you finish him off. I gotta get back to my family."

When he turned to leave, Felix spoke up.

"Cash, I told you not to worry about it. We'll just move your people over here and start over."

Cash knew that was not possible. It was bigger than him. He had to be loyal to those who had been loyal to him. If his home had been hit, he knew everyone else had to be in trouble. He had to return home, because without him nobody would know what to do.

"I can't, Felix," he said plainly. "You do what you gotta do, and I'll do what I gotta do."

With that said, he turned around and continued up the stairs. "I'll call you in 48 hours with an update," he told him.

Before he closed the door to the basement, he heard Migo gurgling something.

It was the sound of death.

ABOUT THE AUTHOR

Tigga is an aspiring best-selling novel author, seeking to keep his audience entertained by creating suspenseful and dramatic Urban Novel stories to keep readers on the edge of their seat. A native of Macon, Georgia, his writing career took off with his debut novel, Cash Money, which is part one to this amazing saga. A beginner in his craft, intends to continue writing and fulfilling the desires of those who seek to take an adventurous trip throughout the mean streets of Georgia without literally encountering the prevalent danger.

holds numerous accolades to date, including earning his Bachelor of Science degree in Business Administration, as well as an Associate of Science degree in Small Business Management from Glenville State College. As founder and co-owner to Lost and Found Publishing, LLC, he offers incarcerated authors an opportunity to monetize their creative

works through his company. A formerly incarcerated federal prisoner himself, wishes to inspire individuals vulnerable to the prison system to better themselves in order to make a valuable contribution to society.

Please continue to follow his career as an author and entrepreneur, because he will keep you wanting to know more about what he has to offer.

Follow on

Instagram @Tiggatheeauthor

Facebook @Lost and Found Publishing Or
Email at varjr@lostandfoundpub.com